RAYMOND CARVER was born in Clatskanie, Oregon, in 1938 and grew up in Yakima, Washington State. His father was a saw-mill worker and his mother was a waitress and clerk. He married early and for years writing had to come second to earning a living for his young family, although he did manage to attend John Gardner's creative writing course at Chico State College. During this period he worked as a hospital porter, a textbook editor, a dictionary salesman, a petrol station attendant and a delivery man. These experiences and his own increasingly desperate domestic circumstances were frequently the subject of his poetry and fiction. Although he published a number of small-press books of poetry and one chapbook of fiction in the 1960s and early 1970s, it was not until the appearance of the story collection *Will You Please Be Quiet, Please?* in 1976 that his work began to reach a wider audience. The following year his luck began to change: he gave up alcohol, which had contributed to the collapse of his marriage, and in the same year met the poet Tess Gallagher with whom he shared the last eleven years of his life. He began to write again and was awarded a Guggenheim Fellowship in 1979 and the prestigious Mildred and Harold Strauss Living Award in 1983. During this prolific period he wrote four collections of stories (*What We Talk about When We Talk about Love, Cathedral, Fires* and *Elephant*) and three collections of poetry *Where Water Comes Together with Other Water* and *Ultramarine*, which are published in Britain as *In a Marine Light*, and *A New Path to the Waterfall*, which was published posthumously. Also published posthumously were his Uncollected Writings, *No Heroics, Please* (edited by William Stull). In the last year of his life he chose and revised for the press his Selected Stories, *Where I'm Calling from*, and was honoured by induction into the American Academy of Arts and Letters. He died in August 1988.

This book contains the nine stories and one poem on which Robert Altman has based his film *Short Cuts*.

Also by Raymond Carver and available in Harvill editions

FICTION

Will You Please Be Quiet, Please?
What We Talk about When We Talk about Love
Cathedral
Elephant
Where I'm Calling from

POETRY

In a Marine Light
A New Path to the Waterfall

ESSAYS, POEMS, STORIES

Fires
No Heroics, Please

Raymond Carver

SHORT CUTS

With an Introduction by
Robert Altman

THE HARVILL PRESS
LONDON

First published in Great Britain by Collins Harvill,
an imprint of HarperCollins*Publishers* Ltd, London, in 1993

This edition first published in 1995 by The Harvill Press

9 10 8

A NOTE ON THE TEXT
The stories and poems in *Short Cuts* appear
in the following Raymond Carver collections:

"Jerry and Molly and Sam" and "Will You Please Be Quiet, Please?"
in *Will You Please Be Quiet, Please?*; "Collectors", "Neighbours",
"A Small Good Thing", "So Much Water So Close to Home",
"They're Not Your Husband" and "Vitamins" in *Where I'm Calling from*;
"Tell the Women We're Going" in *"What We Talk about When
We Talk about Love*; "Lemonade" in *A New Path to the Waterfall*.

The Harvill Press
Random House, 20 Vauxhall Bridge Road
London SW1V 2SA

Random House Australia (Pty) Limited
20 Alfred Street, Milsons Point, Sydney
New South Wales 2061, Australia

Random House New Zealand Limited
18 Poland Road, Glenfield
Auckland 10, New Zealand

Random House (Pty) Limited
Isle of Houghton, Corner of Boundary Road & Carse O'Gowrie
Houghton 2198, South Africa

Random House Publishers India Private Limited
301 World Trade Tower, Intercontinental Grand Complex
Barakhamba Lane, New Delhi 110 001, India

Random House UK Ltd Reg. No 954009
www.randomhouse.co.uk/harvill

A CIP catalogue record for this book
is available from the British Library

ISBN 9781860460401 (from January 2007)
ISBN 1860460402

Papers used by Random House Group are natural, recyclable products made from
wood grown in sustainable forests. The manufacturing processes conform to the
environmental regulations of the country of origin.

Printed and bound in Great Britain by Mackays of Chatham

Contents

INTRODUCTION

Corroborating with Carver

RAYMOND CARVER made poetry out of the prosaic. One critic wrote that he "revealed the strangeness concealed behind the banal," but what he really did was capture the wonderful idiosyncrasies of human behavior, the idiosyncrasies that exist amid the randomness of life's experiences. And human behavior, filled with all its mystery and inspiration, has always fascinated me.

I look at all of Carver's work as just one story, for his stories are all occurrences, all about things that just happen to people and cause their lives to take a turn. Maybe the bottom falls out. Maybe they have a near-miss with disaster. Maybe they just have to go on, knowing things they don't really want to know about one another. They're more about what you don't know rather than what you do know, and the reader fills in the gaps, while recognizing the undercurrents.

In formulating the mosaic of the film *Short Cuts*, which is based on these nine stories and the poem "Lemonade," I've tried to do the same thing – to give the audience one look. But the film could go on for ever, because it's like life – lifting the roof off the Weathers' home and seeing Stormy decimate his furniture with a skillsaw, then lifting off another roof, the Kaisers', or the Wymans', or the Shepherds', and seeing some different behavior.

We've taken liberties with Carver's work: characters have crossed over from one story to another; they connect by various linking devices; names may have changed. And though some purists and Carver fans may be upset, this film has been a serious collaboration between the actors, my co-writer Frank Barhydt, and the Carver material in this collection.

When I first spoke to the poet Tess Gallagher, Ray's widow, about wanting to make this film, I told her I wasn't going to be pristine in my approach to Carver and that the stories were going to be scrambled. She instinctively recognized and encouraged this, and said Ray was an admirer of Nashville, that he liked the helplessness of those characters and their ability to manage nevertheless. She also knew that artists in different fields must use their own skills and vision to do their work. Cinematic equivalents of literary material manifest themselves in unexpected ways.

Through the years of writing, shaping and planning *Short Cuts*, through the myriad financial dealings and turnarounds, Tess and I had numerous discussions and conducted a steady correspondence. The way she received information changed my attitude about things, so I feel I've had discussions with Ray through Tess. She's been a real contributor to the film.

I read all of Ray's writings, filtering him through my own process. The film is made of little pieces of his work that form sections of scenes and characters out of the most basic elements of Ray's creations – new but *not* new. Tess and Zoe Trainer, the emotionally displaced mother and daughter played by Annie Ross and Lori Singer, provide the musical bridges in the film – Annie's jazz and Lori's cello. They are characters Frank Barhydt and I invented, but Tess Gallagher felt they were consistent with Ray's characters and could have come out of his story "Vitamins."

Raymond Carver's view of the world, and probably my own, may be termed dark by some. We're connected by similar attitudes about the arbitrary nature of luck in the scheme of things – the Finnegans' child being hit by a car

8

in "A Small, Good Thing"; the Kanes' marriage upheaval resulting from a body being discovered during a fishing trip in "So Much Water So Close to Home."

Somebody wins the lottery. The same day, that person's sister gets killed by a brick falling off a building in Seattle. Those are both the same thing. The lottery was won both ways. The odds of either happening are very much against you and yet they both happened. One got killed and the other got rich; it's the same action.

One of the reasons we transposed the settings from the Pacific Northwest to Southern California was that we wanted to place the action in a vast suburban setting so that it would be fortuitous for the characters to meet. There were logistical considerations as well, but we wanted the linkages to be accidental. The setting is untapped Los Angeles, which is also Carver country, not Hollywood or Beverly Hills – but Downey, Watts, Compton, Pomona, Glendale – American suburbia, the names you hear about on the freeway reports.

We have twenty-two principal actors in the cast – Anne Archer, Bruce Davison, Robert Downey Jr., Peter Gallagher, Buck Henry, Jennifer Jason Leigh, Jack Lemmon, Huey Lewis, Lyle Lovett, Andie MacDowell, Frances McDormand, Matthew Modine, Julianne Moore, Chris Penn, Tim Robbins, Annie Ross, Lori Singer, Madeleine Stowe, Lili Taylor, Lily Tomlin, Tom Waits and Fred Ward – and they brought things to this film I wouldn't have dreamed of, thickening it, enriching it. Part of this I have to attribute to the foundation of *Short Cuts* – the Carver writings.

Only three or four of these actors ever appeared together in the film because each week we began another story, with another family. But we gave the cast all of the original stories, and many went on to read more of Ray's work. The first family we filmed were the Piggotts, Earl and Doreen, played by Tom Waits and Lily Tomlin, in their trailer park and at

9

Johnnie's Broiler, a classic California coffee shop where Doreen waitresses. Their work was so superb that I thought I'd be in trouble, but all of the actors stepped up to that level, going beyond or sideways from my expectations, taking over and redefining their roles.

The characters do a lot of storytelling in the film, telling little stories about their lives. Many of them are Carver stories or paraphrases of Carver stories or inspired by Carver stories, so we always tried to stay as close as possible to his world, given film's collaborative imperative.

The actors also realized that the particulars these Carver people are talking about aren't the main thing. The elements seemed flexible. They could be talking about anything. Which is not to say the language isn't important, but its subject doesn't have to be X, Y or Z. It could be Q or P or H.

It's a matter of who these people are that determines how they respond to what they're saying. It's not what they're saying that causes the scene to happen, but the fact that these characters are playing the scene. So whether they're talking about how to make a peanut butter sandwich or how to murder their neighbor, the content isn't as significant as what these characters feel and do in the situation, as they develop.

Writing and directing are both acts of discovery. In the end, the film is there and the stories are there and one hopes there is a fruitful interaction. Yet in directing *Short Cuts*, certain things came straight out of my own sensibility, which has its differences, and this is as it should be. I know Ray Carver would have understood that I had to go beyond just paying tribute. Something new happened in the film, and maybe that's the truest form of respect.

But it all began here. I was a reader turning these pages. Trying on these lives.

ROBERT ALTMAN
New York City, 1993

SHORT CUTS

Neighbors

BILL AND ARLENE MILLER were a happy couple. But now and then they felt they alone among their circle had been passed by somehow, leaving Bill to attend to his bookkeeping duties and Arlene occupied with secretarial chores. They talked about it sometimes, mostly in comparison with the lives of their neighbors, Harriet and Jim Stone. It seemed to the Millers that the Stones lived a fuller and brighter life. The Stones were always going out for dinner, or entertaining at home, or traveling about the country somewhere in connection with Jim's work.

The Stones lived across the hall from the Millers. Jim was a salesman for a machine-parts firm and often managed to combine business with pleasure trips, and on this occasion the Stones would be away for ten days, first to Cheyenne, then on to St. Louis to visit relatives. In their absence, the Millers would look after the Stones' apartment, feed Kitty, and water the plants.

Bill and Jim shook hands beside the car. Harriet and Arlene held each other by the elbows and kissed lightly on the lips.

"Have fun," Bill said to Harriet.

"We will," said Harriet. "You kids have fun too."

Arlene nodded.

Jim winked at her. "Bye, Arlene. Take good care of the old man."

"I will," Arlene said.

"Have fun," Bill said.

"You bet," Jim said, clipping Bill lightly on the arm. "And thanks again, you guys."

The Stones waved as they drove away, and the Millers waved too.

"Well, I wish it was us," Bill said.

"God knows, we could use a vacation," Arlene said. She took his arm and put it around her waist as they climbed the stairs to their apartment.

After dinner Arlene said, "Don't forget. Kitty gets liver flavor the first night." She stood in the kitchen doorway folding the handmade tablecloth that Harriet had bought for her last year in Santa Fe.

Bill took a deep breath as he entered the Stones' apartment. The air was already heavy and it was vaguely sweet. The sunburst clock over the television said half past eight. He remembered when Harriet had come home with the clock, how she had crossed the hall to show it to Arlene, cradling the brass case in her arms and talking to it through the tissue paper as if it were an infant.

Kitty rubbed her face against his slippers and then turned onto her side, but jumped up quickly as Bill moved to the kitchen and selected one of the stacked cans from the gleaming drainboard. Leaving the cat to pick at her food, he headed for the bathroom. He looked at himself in the mirror and then closed his eyes and then looked again. He opened the medicine chest. He found a container of pills and read the label – *Harriet Stone. One each day as directed* – and slipped it into his pocket. He went back to the kitchen, drew a pitcher of water, and returned to the living room. He finished watering, set the pitcher on the rug, and opened the liquor cabinet. He reached in back for the bottle of Chivas Regal. He took two drinks from the bottle, wiped his lips on his sleeve, and replaced the bottle in the cabinet.

Kitty was on the couch sleeping. He switched off the lights, slowly closing and checking the door. He had the feeling he had left something.

"What kept you?" Arlene said. She sat with her legs turned under her, watching television.

"Nothing. Playing with Kitty," he said, and went over to her and touched her breasts.

"Let's go to bed, honey," he said.

The next day Bill took only ten minutes of the twenty-minute break allotted for the afternoon and left at fifteen minutes before five. He parked the car in the lot just as Arlene hopped down from the bus. He waited until she entered the building, then ran up the stairs to catch her as she stepped out of the elevator.

"Bill! God, you scared me. You're early," she said.

He shrugged. "Nothing to do at work," he said.

She let him use her key to open the door. He looked at the door across the hall before following her inside.

"Let's go to bed," he said.

"Now?" She laughed. "What's gotten into you?"

"Nothing. Take your dress off." He grabbed for her awkwardly, and she said, "Good God, Bill."

He unfastened his belt.

Later they sent out for Chinese food, and when it arrived they ate hungrily, without speaking, and listened to records.

"Let's not forget to feed Kitty," she said.

"I was just thinking about that," he said. "I'll go right over."

*   *   *

He selected a can of fish flavor for the cat, then filled the pitcher and went to water. When he returned to the kitchen, the cat was scratching in her box. She looked at him steadily before she turned back to the litter. He opened all the cupboards and examined the canned goods, the cereals, the packaged foods, the cocktail and wine glasses, the china, the pots and pans. He opened the refrigerator. He sniffed some celery, took two bites of cheddar cheese, and chewed on an apple as he walked into the bedroom. The bed seemed enormous, with a fluffy white bedspread draped to the floor. He pulled out a nightstand drawer, found a half-empty package of cigarettes and stuffed them into his pocket. Then he stepped to the closet and was opening it when the knock sounded at the front door.

He stopped by the bathroom and flushed the toilet on his way.

"What's been keeping you?" Arlene said. "You've been over here more than an hour."

"Have I really?" he said.

"Yes, you have," she said.

"I had to go to the toilet," he said.

"You have your own toilet," she said.

"I couldn't wait," he said.

That night they made love again.

In the morning he had Arlene call in for him. He showered, dressed, and made a light breakfast. He tried to start a book. He went out for a walk and felt better. But after a while, hands still in his pockets, he returned to the apartment. He stopped at the Stones' door on the chance he might hear the cat moving about. Then he let himself in at his own door and went to the kitchen for the key.

Inside it seemed cooler than his apartment, and darker too.

He wondered if the plants had something to do with the temperature of the air. He looked out the window, and then he moved slowly through each room considering everything that fell under his gaze, carefully, one object at a time. He saw ashtrays, items of furniture, kitchen utensils, the clock. He saw everything. At last he entered the bedroom, and the cat appeared at his feet. He stroked her once, carried her into the bathroom, and shut the door.

He lay down on the bed and stared at the ceiling. He lay for a while with his eyes closed, and then he moved his hand under his belt. He tried to recall what day it was. He tried to remember when the Stones were due back, and then he wondered if they would ever return. He could not remember their faces or the way they talked and dressed. He sighed and with effort rolled off the bed to lean over the dresser and look at himself in the mirror.

He opened the closet and selected a Hawaiian shirt. He looked until he found Bermudas, neatly pressed and hanging over a pair of brown twill slacks. He shed his own clothes and slipped into the shorts and the shirt. He looked in the mirror again. He went to the living room and poured himself a drink and sipped it on his way back to the bedroom. He put on a blue shirt, a dark suit, a blue and white tie, black wing-tip shoes. The glass was empty and he went for another drink.

In the bedroom again, he sat on a chair, crossed his legs, and smiled, observing himself in the mirror. The telephone rang twice and fell silent. He finished the drink and took off the suit. He rummaged through the top drawers until he found a pair of panties and a brassiere. He stepped into the panties and fastened the brassiere, then looked through the closet for an outfit. He put on a black and white checkered skirt and tried to zip it up. He put on a burgundy blouse that buttoned up the front. He considered her shoes, but understood they would not fit. For a long time he looked out the living-room window from behind the curtain. Then he returned to the bedroom and put everything away.

He was not hungry. She did not eat much, either. They looked at each other shyly and smiled. She got up from the table and checked that the key was on the shelf and then she quickly cleared the dishes.

He stood in the kitchen doorway and smoked a cigarette and watched her pick up the key.

"Make yourself comfortable while I go across the hall," she said. "Read the paper or something." She closed her fingers over the key. He was, she said, looking tired.

He tried to concentrate on the news. He read the paper and turned on the television. Finally he went across the hall. The door was locked.

"It's me. Are you still there, honey?" he called.

After a time the lock released and Arlene stepped outside and shut the door. "Was I gone so long?" she said.

"Well, you were," he said.

"Was I?" she said. "I guess I must have been playing with Kitty."

He studied her, and she looked away, her hand still resting on the doorknob.

"It's funny," she said. "You know – to go in someone's place like that."

He nodded, took her hand from the knob, and guided her toward their own door. He let them into their apartment.

"It *is* funny," he said.

He noticed white lint clinging to the back of her sweater, and the color was high in her cheeks. He began kissing her on the neck and hair and she turned and kissed him back.

"Oh, damn," she said. "Damn, damn," she sang, girlishly

clapping her hands. "I just remembered. I really and truly forgot to do what I went over there to do. I didn't feed Kitty or do any watering." She looked at him. "Isn't that stupid?"

"I don't think so," he said. "Just a minute. I'll get my cigarettes and go back with you."

She waited until he had closed and locked their door, and then she took his arm at the muscle and said. "I guess I should tell you. I found some pictures."

He stopped in the middle of the hall. "What kind of pictures?"

"You can see for yourself," she said, and she watched him.

"No kidding." He grinned. "Where?"

"In a drawer," she said.

"No kidding," he said.

And then she said, "Maybe they won't come back," and was at once astonished at her words.

"It could happen," he said. "Anything could happen."

"Or maybe they'll come back and . . ." but she did not finish.

They held hands for the short walk across the hall, and when he spoke she could barely hear his voice.

"The key," he said. "Give it to me."

"What?" she said. She gazed at the door.

"The key," he said. "You have the key."

"My God," she said, "I left the key inside."

He tried the knob. It was locked. Then she tried the knob. It would not turn. Her lips were parted, and her breathing was hard, expectant. He opened his arms and she moved into them.

"Don't worry," he said into her ear. "For God's sake, don't worry."

They stayed there. They held each other. They leaned into the door as if against a wind, and braced themselves.

They're Not Your Husband

EARL OBER WAS BETWEEN JOBS as a salesman. But Doreen, his wife, had gone to work nights as a waitress at a twenty-four-hour coffee shop at the edge of town. One night, when he was drinking, Earl decided to stop by the coffee shop and have something to eat. He wanted to see where Doreen worked, and he wanted to see if he could order something on the house.

He sat at the counter and studied the menu.

"What are you doing here?" Doreen said when she saw him sitting there.

She handed over an order to the cook. "What are you going to order, Earl?" she said. "The kids okay?"

"They're fine," Earl said. "I'll have coffee and one of those Number Two sandwiches."

Doreen wrote it down.

"Any chance of, you know?" he said to her and winked.

"No," she said. "Don't talk to me now. I'm busy."

Earl drank his coffee and waited for the sandwich. Two men in business suits, their ties undone, their collars open, sat down next to him and asked for coffee. As Doreen walked away with the coffeepot, one of the men said to the other, "Look at the ass on that. I don't believe it."

The other man laughed. "I've seen better," he said.

"That's what I mean," the first man said. "But some jokers like their quim fat."

"Not me," the other man said.

"Not me, neither," the first man said. "That's what I was saying."

Doreen put the sandwich in front of Earl. Around the sandwich there were French fries, coleslaw, dill pickle.

"Anything else?" she said. "A glass of milk?"

He didn't say anything. He shook his head when she kept standing there.

"I'll get you more coffee," she said.

She came back with the pot and poured coffee for him and for the two men. Then she picked up a dish and turned to get some ice cream. She reached down into the container and with the dipper began to scoop up the ice cream. The white skirt yanked against her hips and crawled up her legs. What showed was girdle, and it was pink, thighs that were rumpled and gray and a little hairy, and veins that spread in a berserk display.

The two men sitting beside Earl exchanged looks. One of them raised his eyebrows. The other man grinned and kept looking at Doreen over his cup as she spooned chocolate syrup over the ice cream. When she began shaking the can of whipped cream, Earl got up, leaving his food, and headed for the door. He heard her call his name, but he kept going.

He checked on the children and then went to the other bedroom and took off his clothes. He pulled the covers up, closed his eyes, and allowed himself to think. The feeling started in his face and worked down into his stomach and legs. He opened his eyes and rolled his head back and forth on the pillow. Then he turned on his side and fell asleep.

In the morning, after she had sent the children off to school, Doreen came into the bedroom and raised the shade. Earl was already awake.

"Look at yourself in the mirror," he said.

"What?" she said. "What are you talking about?"

"Just look at yourself in the mirror," he said.

"What am I supposed to see?" she said. But she looked in the mirror over the dresser and pushed the hair away from her shoulders.

"Well?" he said.

"Well, what?" she said.

"I hate to say anything," Earl said, "but I think you better give a diet some thought. I mean it. I'm serious. I think you could lose a few pounds. Don't get mad."

"What are you saying?" she said.

"Just what I said. I think you could lose a few pounds. A few pounds, anyway," he said.

"You never said anything before," she said. She raised her nightgown over her hips and turned to look at her stomach in the mirror.

"I never felt it was a problem before," he said. He tried to pick his words.

The nightgown still gathered around her waist, Doreen turned her back to the mirror and looked over her shoulder. She raised one buttock in her hand and let it drop.

Earl closed his eyes. "Maybe I'm all wet," he said.

"I guess I could afford to lose. But it'd be hard," she said.

"You're right, it won't be easy," he said. "But I'll help."

"Maybe you're right," she said. She dropped her nightgown and looked at him and then she took her nightgown off.

They talked about diets. They talked about the protein diets, the vegetable-only diets, the grapefruit-juice diets. But they decided they didn't have the money to buy the steaks the protein diet called for. And Doreen said she didn't care for all that many vegetables. And since she didn't like

22

grapefruit juice that much, she didn't see how she could do that one, either.

"Okay, forget it," he said.

"No, you're right," she said. "I'll do something."

"What about exercises?" he said.

"I'm getting all the exercise I need down there," she said.

"Just quit eating," Earl said. "For a few days, anyway."

"All right," she said. "I'll try. For a few days I'll give it a try. You've convinced me."

"I'm a closer," Earl said.

He figured up the balance in their checking account, then drove to the discount store and bought a bathroom scale. He looked the clerk over as she rang up the sale.

At home he had Doreen take off all her clothes and get on the scale. He frowned when he saw the veins. He ran his finger the length of one that sprouted up her thigh.

"What are you doing?" she asked.

"Nothing," he said.

He looked at the scale and wrote the figure down on a piece of paper.

"All right," Earl said. "All right."

The next day he was gone for most of the afternoon on an interview. The employer, a heavyset man who limped as he showed Earl around the plumbing fixtures in the warehouse, asked if Earl were free to travel.

"You bet I'm free," Earl said.

The man nodded.

Earl smiled.

He could hear the television before he opened the door to the house. The children did not look up as he walked through the living room. In the kitchen, Doreen, dressed for work, was eating scrambled eggs and bacon.

"What are you doing?" Earl said.

She continued to chew the food, cheeks puffed. But then she spit everything into a napkin.

"I couldn't help myself," she said.

"Slob," Earl said. "*Go ahead, eat! Go on!*" He went to the bedroom, closed the door, and lay on the covers. He could still hear the television. He put his hands behind his head and stared at the ceiling.

She opened the door.

"I'm going to try again," Doreen said.

"Okay," he said.

Two mornings later she called him into the bathroom. "Look," she said.

He read the scale. He opened a drawer and took out the paper and read the scale again while she grinned.

"Three-quarters of a pound," she said.

"It's something," he said and patted her hip.

He read the classifieds. He went to the state employment office. Every three or four days he drove someplace for an interview, and at night he counted her tips. He smoothed out the dollar bills on the table and stacked the nickels, dimes, and quarters in piles of one dollar each. Each morning he put her on the scale.

In two weeks she had lost three and a half pounds.

"I pick," she said. "I starve myself all day, and then I pick at work. It adds up."

But a week later she had lost five pounds. The week after that, nine and a half pounds. Her clothes were loose on her. She had to cut into the rent money to buy a new uniform.

"People are saying things at work," she said.

"What kind of things?" Earl said.

"That I'm too pale, for one thing," she said. "That I don't look like myself. They're afraid I'm losing too much weight."

"What is wrong with losing?" he said. "Don't you pay any attention to them. Tell them to mind their own business. They're not your husband. You don't have to live with them."

"I have to work with them," Doreen said.

"That's right," Earl said. "But they're not your husband."

Each morning he followed her into the bathroom and waited while she stepped onto the scale. He got down on his knees with a pencil and the piece of paper. The paper was covered with dates, days of the week, numbers. He read the number on the scale, consulted the paper, and either nodded his head or pursed his lips.

Doreen spent more time in bed now. She went back to bed after the children had left for school, and she napped in the afternoons before going to work. Earl helped around the house, watched television, and let her sleep. He did all the shopping, and once in a while he went on an interview.

One night he put the children to bed, turned off the television, and decided to go for a few drinks. When the bar closed, he drove to the coffee shop.

He sat at the counter and waited. When she saw him, she said, "Kids okay?"

Earl nodded.

He took his time ordering. He kept looking at her as she moved up and down behind the counter. He finally ordered a cheeseburger. She gave the order to the cook and went to wait on someone else.

Another waitress came by with a coffeepot and filled Earl's cup.

"Who's your friend?" he said and nodded at his wife.

"Her name's Doreen," the waitress said.

"She looks a lot different than the last time I was in here," he said.

"I wouldn't know," the waitress said.

He ate the cheeseburger and drank the coffee. People kept sitting down and getting up at the counter. Doreen waited on most of the people at the counter, though now and then the other waitress came along to take an order. Earl watched his wife and listened carefully. Twice he had to leave his place to go to the bathroom. Each time he wondered if he might have missed hearing something. When he came back the second time, he found his cup gone and someone in his place. He took a stool at the end of the counter next to an older man in a striped shirt.

"What do you want?" Doreen said to Earl when she saw him again. "Shouldn't you be home?"

"Give me some coffee," he said.

The man next to Earl was reading a newspaper. He looked up and watched Doreen pour Earl a cup of coffee. He glanced at Doreen as she walked away. Then he went back to his newspaper.

Earl sipped his coffee and waited for the man to say something. He watched the man out of the corner of his eye. The man had finished eating and his plate was pushed to the side. The man lit a cigarette, folded the newspaper in front of him, and continued to read.

Doreen came by and removed the dirty plate and poured the man more coffee.

"What do you think of that?" Earl said to the man, nodding at Doreen as she moved down the counter. "Don't you think that's something special?"

The man looked up. He looked at Doreen and then at Earl, and then went back to his newspaper.

"Well, what do you think?" Earl said. "I'm asking. Does it look good or not? Tell me."

The man rattled the newspaper.

When Doreen started down the counter again, Earl nudged the man's shoulder and said, "I'm telling you something. Listen. Look at the ass on her. Now you watch this now. Could I have a chocolate sundae?" Earl called to Doreen.

She stopped in front of him and let out her breath. Then she turned and picked up a dish and the ice-cream dipper. She leaned over the freezer, reached down, and began to press the dipper into the ice cream. Earl looked at the man and winked as Doreen's skirt traveled up her thighs. But the man's eyes caught the eyes of the other waitress. And then the man put the newspaper under his arm and reached into his pocket.

The other waitress came straight to Doreen. "Who is this character?" she said.

"Who?" Doreen said and looked around with the ice-cream dish in her hand.

"Him," the other waitress said and nodded at Earl. "Who is this joker, anyway?"

Earl put on his best smile. He held it. He held it until he felt his face pulling out of shape.

But the other waitress just studied him, and Doreen began to shake her head slowly. The man had put some change beside his cup and stood up, but he too waited to hear the answer. They all stared at Earl.

"He's a salesman. He's my husband," Doreen said at last, shrugging. Then she put the unfinished chocolate sundae in front of him and went to total up his check.

Vitamins

I HAD A JOB and Patti didn't. I worked a few hours a night
for the hospital. It was a nothing job. I did some work, signed
the card for eight hours, went drinking with the nurses. After
a while, Patti wanted a job. She said she needed a job for her
self-respect. So she started selling multiple vitamins door to
door.

For a while, she was just another girl who went up and
down blocks in strange neighborhoods, knocking on doors.
But she learned the ropes. She was quick and had excelled
at things in school. She had personality. Pretty soon the com-
pany gave her a promotion. Some of the girls who weren't
doing so hot were put to work under her. Before long, she
had herself a crew and a little office out in the mall. But the
girls who worked for her were always changing. Some
would quit after a couple of days – after a couple of hours,
sometimes. But sometimes there were girls who were good
at it. They could sell vitamins. These were the girls that stuck
with Patti. They formed the core of the crew. But there were
girls who couldn't give away vitamins.

The girls who couldn't cut it would just quit. Just not
show up for work. If they had a phone, they'd take it off
the hook. They wouldn't answer the door. Patti took these
losses to heart, like the girls were new converts who had lost
their way. She blamed herself. But she got over it. There
were too many not to get over it.

Once in a while a girl would freeze and not be able to push the doorbell. Or maybe she'd get to the door and something would happen to her voice. Or she'd get the greeting mixed up with something she shouldn't be saying until she got inside. A girl like this, she'd decide to pack it in, take the sample case, head for the car, hang around until Patti and the others finished. There'd be a conference. Then they'd all ride back to the office. They'd say things to buck themselves up. "When the going gets tough, the tough get going." And, "Do the right things and the right things will happen." Things like that.

Sometimes a girl just disappeared in the field, sample case and all. She'd hitch a ride into town, then beat it. But there were always girls to take her place. Girls were coming and going in those days. Patti had a list. Every few weeks she'd run a little ad in *The Pennysaver*. There'd be more girls and more training. There was no end of girls.

The core group was made up of Patti, Donna, and Sheila. Patti was a looker. Donna and Sheila were only medium-pretty. One night this Sheila said to Patti that she loved her more than anything on earth. Patti told me these were the words. Patti had driven Sheila home and they were sitting in front of Sheila's place. Patti said to Sheila she loved her, too. Patti said to Sheila she loved all her girls. But not in the way Sheila had in mind. Then Sheila touched Patti's breast. Patti said she took Sheila's hand and held it. She said she told her she didn't swing that way. She said Sheila didn't bat an eye, that she only nodded, held on to Patti's hand, kissed it, and got out of the car.

That was around Christmas. The vitamin business was pretty bad off back then, so we thought we'd have a party to cheer everybody up. It seemed like a good idea at the time. Sheila

was the first to get drunk and pass out. She passed out on her feet, fell over, and didn't wake up for hours. One minute she was standing in the middle of the living room, then her eyes closed, the legs buckled, and she went down with a glass in her hand. The hand holding the drink smacked the coffee table when she fell. She didn't make a sound otherwise. The drink poured out onto the rug. Patti and I and somebody else lugged her out to the back porch and put her down on a cot and did what we could to forget about her.

Everybody got drunk and went home. Patti went to bed. I wanted to keep on, so I sat at the table with a drink until it began to get light out. Then Sheila came in from the porch and started up. She said she had this headache that was so bad it was like somebody was sticking wires in her brain. She said it was such a bad headache she was afraid it was going to leave her with a permanent squint. And she was sure her little finger was broken. She showed it to me. It looked purple. She bitched about us letting her sleep all night with her contacts in. She wanted to know didn't anybody give a shit. She brought the finger up close and looked at it. She shook her head. She held the finger as far away as she could and looked some more. It was like she couldn't believe the things that must have happened to her that night. Her face was puffy, and her hair was all over. She ran cold water on her finger. "God. Oh, God," she said and cried some over the sink. But she'd made a serious pass at Patti, a declaration of love. and I didn't have any sympathy.

I was drinking Scotch and milk with a sliver of ice. Sheila was leaning on the drainboard. She watched me from her little slits of eyes. I took some of my drink. I didn't say anything. She went back to telling me how bad she felt. She said she needed to see a doctor. She said she was going to

VITAMINS

wake Patti. She said she was quitting, leaving the state, going
to Portland. That she had to say goodbye to Patti first. She
kept on. She wanted Patti to drive her to the hospital for her
finger and her eyes.

"I'll drive you," I said. I didn't want to do it, but I would.

"I want Patti to drive me," Sheila said.

She was holding the wrist of her bad hand with her good
hand, the little finger as big as a pocket flashlight. "Besides,
we need to talk. I need to tell her I'm going to Portland. I
need to say goodbye."

I said, "I guess I'll have to tell her for you. She's asleep."

Sheila turned mean. "We're *friends*," she said. "I have to
talk to her. I have to tell her myself."

I shook my head. "She's asleep. I just said so."

"We're friends and we love each other," Sheila said. "I
have to say goodbye to her."

Sheila made to leave the kitchen.

I started to get up. I said, "I said I'll drive you."

"You're drunk! You haven't even been to bed yet." She
looked at her finger again and said, "Goddamn, why'd this
have to happen?"

"Not too drunk to drive you to the hospital," I said.

"I won't ride with you!" Sheila yelled.

"Suit yourself. But you're not going to wake Patti. Lesbo
bitch," I said.

"Bastard," she said.

That's what she said, and then she went out of the kitchen
and out the front door without using the bathroom or even
washing her face. I got up and looked through the window.
She was walking down the road toward Euclid. Nobody else
was up. It was too early.

I finished my drink and thought about fixing another one.
I fixed it.

Nobody saw any more of Sheila after that. None of us

31

vitamin-related people, anyway. She walked to Euclid Avenue and out of our lives.

Later on Patti said, "What happened to Sheila?" and I said, "She went to Portland."

I had the hots for Donna, the other member of the core group. We'd danced to some Duke Ellington records that night of the party. I'd held her pretty tight, smelled her hair, kept a hand low on her back as I moved her over the rug. It was great dancing with her. I was the only fellow at the party, and there were seven girls, six of them dancing with each other. It was great just looking around the living room.

I was in the kitchen when Donna came in with her empty glass. We were alone for a bit. I got her into a little embrace. She hugged me back. We stood there and hugged.

Then she said, "Don't. Not now."

When I heard that "Not now," I let go. I figured it was money in the bank.

I'd been at the table thinking about that hug when Sheila came in with her finger.

I thought some more about Donna. I finished the drink. I took the phone off the hook and headed for the bedroom. I took off my clothes and got in next to Patti. I lay for a while, winding down. Then I started in. But she didn't wake up. Afterward, I closed my eyes.

It was the afternoon when I opened them again. I was in bed alone. Rain was blowing against the window. A sugar doughnut was lying on Patti's pillow, and a glass of old water was on the nightstand. I was still drunk and couldn't figure anything out. I knew it was Sunday and close to Christmas. I ate the doughnut and drank the water. I went back to sleep until I heard Patti running the vacuum. She came into the bedroom and asked about Sheila. That's when I told her, said she'd gone to Portland.

A week or so into the new year, Patti and I were having a drink. She'd just come home from work. It wasn't so late, but it was dark and rainy. I was going to work in a couple of hours. But first we were having us some Scotch and talking. Patti was tired. She was down in the dumps and into her third drink. Nobody was buying vitamins. All she had was Donna and Pam, a semi-new girl who was a klepto. We were talking about things like negative weather and the number of parking tickets you could get away with. Then we got to talking about how we'd be better off if we moved to Arizona, someplace like that.

I fixed us another one. I looked out the window. Arizona wasn't a bad idea.

Patti said, "Vitamins." She picked up her glass and spun the ice. "For shit's sake!" she said. "I mean, when I was a girl, this is the last thing I ever saw myself doing. Jesus, I never thought I'd grow up to sell vitamins. Door-to-door vitamins. This beats all. This really blows my mind."

"I never thought so either, honey," I said.

"That's right," she said. "You said it in a nutshell."

"Honey."

"Don't honey me," she said. "This is hard, brother. This life is not easy, any way you cut it."

She seemed to think things over for a bit. She shook her head. Then she finished her drink. She said, "I even dream of vitamins when I'm asleep. I don't have any relief. There's no relief! At least you can walk away from your job and leave it behind. I'll bet you haven't had one dream about it. I'll bet you don't dream about waxing floors or whatever you do down there. After you've left the goddamn place, you don't come home and dream about it, do you?" she screamed.

I said, "I can't remember what I dream. Maybe I don't dream. I don't remember anything when I wake up." I shrugged. I didn't keep track of what went on in my head when I was asleep. I didn't care.

"You dream!" Patti said. "Even if you don't remember. Everybody dreams. If you didn't dream, you'd go crazy. I read about it. It's an outlet. People dream when they're asleep. Or else they'd go nuts. But when I dream, I dream of vitamins. Do you see what I'm saying?" She had her eyes fixed on me.

"Yes and no," I said.

It wasn't a simple question.

"I dream I'm pitching vitamins," she said. "I'm selling vitamins day and night. Jesus, what a life," she said.

She finished her drink.

"How's Pam doing?" I said. "She still stealing things?" I wanted to get us off this subject. But there wasn't anything else I could think of.

Patti said, "Shit," and shook her head like I didn't know anything. We listened to it rain.

"Nobody's selling vitamins," Patti said. She picked up her glass. But it was empty. "Nobody's buying vitamins. That's what I'm telling you. Didn't you hear me?"

I got up to fix us another. "Donna doing anything?" I said. I read the label on the bottle and waited.

Patti said, "She made a little sale two days ago. That's all. That's all that any of us has done this week. It wouldn't surprise me if she quit. I wouldn't blame her," Patti said. "If I was in her place, I'd quit. But if she quits, then what? Then I'm back at the start, that's what. Ground zero. Middle of winter, people sick all over the state, people dying, and nobody thinks they need vitamins. I'm sick as hell myself."

"What's wrong, honey?" I put the drinks on the table and sat down. She went on like I hadn't said anything. Maybe I hadn't.

"I'm my only customer," she said. "I think taking all these vitamins is doing something to my skin. Does my skin look okay to you? Can a person get overdosed on vitamins? I'm getting to where I can't even take a crap like a normal person."

"Honey," I said.

Patti said, "You don't care if I take vitamins. That's the point. You don't care about anything. The windshield wiper quit this afternoon in the rain. I almost had a wreck. I came this close."

We went on drinking and talking until it was time for me to go to work. Patti said she was going to soak in a tub if she didn't fall asleep first. "I'm asleep on my feet," she said. She said, "Vitamins. That's all there is anymore." She looked around the kitchen. She looked at her empty glass. She was drunk. But she let me kiss her. Then I left for work.

There was a place I went to after work. I'd started going for the music and because I could get a drink there after closing hours. It was a place called the Off-Broadway. It was a spade place in a spade neighborhood. It was run by a spade named Khaki. People would show up after the other places had stopped serving. They'd ask for house specials – RC Colas with a shooter of whiskey – or else they'd bring in their own stuff under their coats, order RC, and build their own. Musicians showed up to jam, and the drinkers who wanted to keep drinking came to drink and listen to the music. Sometimes people danced. But mainly they sat around and drank and listened.

Now and then a spade hit a spade in the head with a bottle.

A story went around once that somebody had followed somebody into the Gents and cut the man's throat while he had his hands down pissing. But I never saw any trouble. Nothing that Khaki couldn't handle. Khaki was a big spade with a bald head that lit up weird under the fluorescents. He wore Hawaiian shirts that hung over his pants. I think he carried something inside his waistband. At least a sap, maybe. If somebody started to get out of line, Khaki would go over to where it was beginning. He'd rest his big hand on the party's shoulder and say a few words and that was that. I'd been going there off and on for months. I was pleased that he'd say things to me, things like, "How're you doing tonight, friend?" Or, "Friend, I haven't seen you for a spell."

The Off-Broadway is where I took Donna on our date. It was the one date we ever had.

I'd walked out of the hospital just after midnight. It'd cleared up and stars were out. I still had this buzz on from the Scotch I'd had with Patti. But I was thinking to hit Birney's for a quick one on the way home. Donna's car was parked in the space next to my car, and Donna was inside the car. I remembered that hug we'd had in the kitchen. "Not now," she'd said.

She rolled the window down and knocked ashes from her cigarette.

"I couldn't sleep," she said. "I have some things on my mind, and I couldn't sleep."

I said, "Donna. Hey, I'm glad to see you, Donna."

"I don't know what's wrong with me," she said.

"You want to go someplace for a drink?" I said.

"Patti's my friend," she said.

"She's my friend, too," I said. Then I said, "Let's go."

"Just so you know," she said.

"There's this place. It's a spade place," I said. "They have music. We can get a drink, listen to some music."

"You want to drive me?" Donna said.

I said, "Scoot over."

She started right in about vitamins. Vitamins were on the skids, vitamins had taken a nose dive. The bottom had fallen out of the vitamin market.

Donna said, "I hate to do this to Patti. She's my best friend, and she's trying to build things up for us. But I may have to quit. This is between us. Swear it! But I have to eat. I have to pay rent. I need new shoes and a new coat. Vitamins can't cut it," Donna said. "I don't think vitamins is where it's at anymore. I haven't said anything to Patti. Like I said, I'm still just thinking about it."

Donna laid her hand next to my leg. I reached down and squeezed her fingers. She squeezed back. Then she took her hand away and pushed in the lighter. After she had her cigarette going, she put the hand back. "Worse than anything, I hate to let Patti down. You know what I'm saying? We were a team." She reached me her cigarette. "I know it's a different brand," she said, "but try it, go ahead."

I pulled into the lot for the Off-Broadway. Three spades were up against an old Chrysler that had a cracked windshield. They were just lounging, passing a bottle in a sack. They looked us over. I got out and went around to open up for Donna. I checked the doors, took her arm, and we headed for the street. The spades just watched us.

I said, "You're not thinking about moving to Portland, are you?"

We were on the sidewalk. I put my arm around her waist.

"I don't know anything about Portland. Portland hasn't crossed my mind once."

The front half of the Off-Broadway was like a regular café

and bar. A few spades sat at the counter and a few more worked over plates of food at tables with red oilcloth. We went through the café and into the big room in back. There was a long counter with booths against the wall and farther back a platform where musicians could set up. In front of the platform was what passed for a dance floor. The bars and nightclubs were still serving, so people hadn't turned up in any real numbers yet. I helped Donna take off her coat. We picked a booth and put our cigarettes on the table. The spade waitress named Hannah came over. Hannah and me nodded. She looked at Donna. I ordered us two RC specials and decided to feel good about things.

After the drinks came and I'd paid and we'd each had a sip, we started hugging. We carried on like this for a while, squeezing and patting, kissing each other's face. Every so often Donna would stop and draw back, push me away a little, then hold me by the wrists. She'd gaze into my eyes. Then her lids would close slowly and we'd fall to kissing again. Pretty soon the place began to fill up. We stopped kissing. But I kept my arm around her. She put her fingers on my leg. A couple of spade horn-players and a white drummer began fooling around with something. I figured Donna and me would have another drink and listen to the set. Then we'd leave and go to her place to finish things.

I'd just ordered two more from Hannah when this spade named Benny came over with this other spade – this big, dressed-up spade. This big spade had little red eyes and was wearing a three-piece pinstripe. He had on a rose-colored shirt, a tie, a topcoat, a fedora – all of it.

"How's my man?" said Benny.

Benny stuck out his hand for a brother handshake. Benny and I had talked. He knew I liked the music, and he used to come over to talk whenever we were both in the place. He liked to talk about Johnny Hodges, how he'd played sax backup for Johnny. He'd say things like, "When Johnny and me had this gig in Mason City."

"Hi, Benny," I said.

"I want you to meet Nelson," Benny said. "He just back from Nam today. This morning. He here to listen to some of these good sounds. He got on his dancing shoes in case." Benny looked at Nelson and nodded. "This here is Nelson."

I was looking at Nelson's shiny shoes, and then I looked at Nelson. He seemed to want to place me from somewhere. He studied me. Then he let loose a rolling grin that showed his teeth.

"This is Donna," I said. "Donna, this is Benny, and this is Nelson. Nelson, this is Donna."

"Hello, girl," Nelson said, and Donna said right back, "Hello there, Nelson. Hello, Benny."

"Maybe we'll just slide in and join you folks?" Benny said. "Okay?"

I said, "Sure."

But I was sorry they hadn't found someplace else.

"We're not going to be here long," I said. "Just long enough to finish this drink, is all."

"I know, man, I know," Benny said. He sat across from me after Nelson had let himself down into the booth. "Things to do, places to go. Yes sir, Benny knows," Benny said, and winked.

Nelson looked across the booth to Donna. Then he took off the hat. He seemed to be looking for something on the brim as he turned the hat around in his big hands. He made room for the hat on the table. He looked up at Donna. He grinned and squared his shoulders. He had to square his shoulders every few minutes. It was like he was very tired of carrying them around.

"You real good friends with him, I bet," Nelson said to Donna.

"We're good friends," Donna said.

Hannah came over. Benny asked for RCs. Hannah went away, and Nelson worked a pint of whiskey from his topcoat.

"Good friends," Nelson said. "Real good friends." He unscrewed the cap on his whiskey.

"Watch it, Nelson," Benny said. "Keep that out of sight. Nelson just got off the plane from Nam," Benny said.

Nelson raised the bottle and drank some of his whiskey. He screwed the cap back on, laid the bottle on the table, and put his hat down on top of it. "Real good friends," he said.

Benny looked at me and rolled his eyes. But he was drunk, too. "I got to get into shape," he said to me. He drank RC from both of their glasses and then held the glasses under the table and poured whiskey. He put the bottle in his coat pocket. "Man, I ain't put my lips to a reed for a month now. I got to get with it."

We were bunched in the booth, glasses in front of us, Nelson's hat on the table. "You," Nelson said to me. "You with somebody else, ain't you? This beautiful woman, she ain't your wife. I know that. But you real good friends with this woman. Ain't I right?"

I had some of my drink. I couldn't taste the whiskey. I couldn't taste anything. I said, "Is all that shit about Vietnam true we see on the TV?"

Nelson had his red eyes fixed on me. He said, "What I want to say is, do you know where your wife is? I bet she out with some dude and she be seizing his nipples for him and pulling his pud for him while you setting here big as life with your good friend. I bet she have herself a good friend, too."

"Nelson," Benny said.

"Nelson nothing," Nelson said.

Benny said, "Nelson, let's leave these people be. There's

somebody in that other booth. Somebody I told you about. Nelson just this morning got off a plane," Benny said.

"I bet I know what you thinking," Nelson said. "I bet you thinking, 'Now here a big drunk nigger and what am I going to do with him? Maybe I have to whip his ass for him!' That what you thinking?"

I looked around the room. I saw Khaki standing near the platform, the musicians working away behind him. Some dancers were on the floor. I thought Khaki looked right at me – but if he did, he looked away again.

"Ain't it your turn to talk?" Nelson said. "I just teasing you. I ain't done any teasing since I left Nam. I teased the gooks some." He grinned again, his big lips rolling back. Then he stopped grinning and just stared.

"Show them that ear," Benny said. He put his glass on the table. "Nelson got himself an ear off one of them little dudes," Benny said. "He carry it with him. Show them, Nelson."

Nelson sat there. Then he started feeling the pockets of his topcoat. He took things out of one pocket. He took out some keys and a box of cough drops.

Donna said, "I don't want to see an ear. Ugh. Double ugh. Jesus." She looked at me.

"We have to go," I said.

Nelson was still feeling in his pockets. He took a wallet from a pocket inside the suit coat and put it on the table. He patted the wallet. "Five big ones there. Listen here," he said to Donna. "I going to give you two bills. You with me? I give you two big ones, and then you French me. Just like his woman doing some other big fellow. You hear? You know she got her mouth on somebody's hammer right this minute while he here with his hand up your skirt. Fair's fair. Here." He pulled the corners of the bills from his wallet. "Hell, here another hundred for your good friend, so he won't feel left out. He don't have to do nothing. You don't have to do nothing," Nelson said to me. "You just sit there and drink your drink and listen to the music. Good music. Me and this woman walk out together like good friends. And she walk back in by herself. Won't be long, she be back."

"Nelson," Benny said, "this is no way to talk, Nelson."

Nelson grinned. "I finished talking," he said.

He found what he'd been feeling for. It was a silver cigarette case. He opened it up. I looked at the ear inside. It sat on a bed of cotton. It looked like a dried mushroom. But it was a real ear, and it was hooked up to a key chain.

"Jesus," said Donna. "Yuck."

"Ain't that something?" Nelson said. He was watching Donna.

"No way. Fuck off," Donna said.

"Girl," Nelson said.

"Nelson," I said. And then Nelson fixed his red eyes on me. He pushed the hat and wallet and cigarette case out of his way.

"What do you want?" Nelson said. "I give you what you want."

Khaki had a hand on my shoulder and the other one on Benny's shoulder. He leaned over the table, his head shining under the lights. "How you folks? You all having fun?"

"Everything all right, Khaki," Benny said. "Everything A-okay. These people here was just fixing to leave. Me and Nelson going to sit and listen to the music."

"That's good," Khaki said. "Folks be happy is my motto."

He looked around the booth. He looked at Nelson's wallet on the table and at the open cigarette case next to the wallet. He saw the ear.

"That a real ear?" Khaki said.

Benny said, "It is. Show him that ear, Nelson. Nelson just stepped off the plane from Nam with this ear. This ear has traveled halfway around the world to be on this table tonight. Nelson, show him," Benny said.

Nelson picked up the case and handed it to Khaki.

Khaki examined the ear. He took up the chain and dangled the ear in front of his face. He looked at it. He let it swing back and forth on the chain. "I heard about these dried-up ears and dicks and such."

"I took it off one of them gooks," Nelson said. "He couldn't hear nothing with it no more. I wanted me a keepsake."

Khaki turned the ear on its chain.

Donna and I began getting out of the booth.

"Girl, don't go," Nelson said.

"Nelson," Benny said.

Khaki was watching Nelson now. I stood beside the booth with Donna's coat. My legs were crazy.

Nelson raised his voice. He said, "You go with this mother here, you let him put his face in your sweets, you both going to have to deal with me."

We started to move away from the booth. People were looking.

"Nelson just got off the plane from Nam this morning," I heard Benny say. "We been drinking all day. This been the longest day on record. But me and him, we going to be fine, Khaki."

Nelson yelled something over the music. He yelled, "It ain't going to do no good! Whatever you do, it ain't going to help none!" I heard him say that, and then I couldn't hear anymore. The music stopped, and then it started again. We didn't look back. We kept going. We got out to the sidewalk.

★　　★　　★

I opened the door for her. I started us back to the hospital. Donna stayed over on her side. She'd used the lighter on a cigarette, but she wouldn't talk.

I tried to say something. I said, "Look, Donna, don't get on a downer because of this. I'm sorry it happened," I said.

"I could of used the money," Donna said. "That's what I was thinking."

I kept driving and didn't look at her.

"It's true," she said. "I could of used the money." She shook her head. "I don't know," she said. She put her chin down and cried.

"Don't cry," I said.

"I'm not going in to work tomorrow, today, whenever it is the alarm goes off," she said. "I'm not going in. I'm leaving town. I take what happened back there as a sign." She pushed in the lighter and waited for it to pop out.

I pulled in beside my car and killed the engine. I looked in the rearview, half thinking I'd see that old Chrysler drive into the lot behind me with Nelson in the seat. I kept my hands on the wheel for a minute, and then dropped them to my lap. I didn't want to touch Donna. The hug we'd given each other in my kitchen that night, the kissing we'd done at the Off-Broadway, that was all over.

I said, "What are you going to do?" But I didn't care. Right then she could have died of a heart attack and it wouldn't have meant anything.

"Maybe I could go up to Portland," she said. "There must be something in Portland. Portland's on everybody's mind these days. Portland's a drawing card. Portland this, Portland that. Portland's as good a place as any. It's all the same."

"Donna," I said, "I'd better go."

I started to let myself out. I cracked the door, and the overhead light came on.

"For Christ's sake, turn off that light!"

I got out in a hurry. "'Night, Donna," I said.

I left her staring at the dashboard. I started up my car and turned on the lights. I slipped it in gear and fed it the gas.

I poured Scotch, drank some of it, and took the glass into the bathroom. I brushed my teeth. Then I pulled open a drawer. Patti yelled something from the bedroom. She opened the bathroom door. She was still dressed. She'd been sleeping with her clothes on, I guess.

"What time is it?" she screamed. "I've overslept! Jesus, oh my God! You've let me oversleep, goddamn you!"

She was wild. She stood in the doorway with her clothes on. She could have been fixing to go to work. But there was no sample case, no vitamins. She was having a bad dream, is all. She began shaking her head from side to side.

I couldn't take any more tonight. "Go back to sleep, honey. I'm looking for something," I said. I knocked some stuff out of the medicine chest. Things rolled into the sink. "Where's the aspirin?" I said. I knocked down some more things. I didn't care. Things kept falling.

Will You Please Be Quiet, Please?

WHEN HE WAS EIGHTEEN and was leaving home for the first time, Ralph Wyman was counseled by his father, principal of Jefferson Elementary School and trumpet soloist in the Weaverville Elks Club Auxiliary Band, that life was a very serious matter, an enterprise insisting on strength and purpose in a young person just setting out, an arduous undertaking, everyone knew that, but nevertheless a rewarding one, Ralph Wyman's father believed and said.

But in college Ralph's goals were hazy. He thought he wanted to be a doctor and he thought he wanted to be a lawyer, and he took pre-medical courses and courses in the history of jurisprudence and business law before he decided he had neither the emotional detachment necessary for medicine nor the ability for sustained reading required in law, especially as such reading might concern property and inheritance. Though he continued to take classes here and there in the sciences and in business, Ralph also took some classes in philosophy and literature and felt himself on the brink of some kind of huge discovery about himself. But it never came. It was during this time – his lowest ebb, as he referred to it later – that Ralph believed he almost had a breakdown; he was in a fraternity and he got drunk every night. He drank so much that he acquired a reputation and was called "Jackson," after the bartender at The Keg.

Then, in his third year, Ralph came under the influence of

a particularly persuasive teacher. Dr. Maxwell was his name; Ralph would never forget him. He was a handsome, graceful man in his early forties, with exquisite manners and with just the trace of the South in his voice. He had been educated at Vanderbilt, had studied in Europe, and had later had something to do with one or two literary magazines back East. Almost overnight, Ralph would later say, he decided on teaching as a career. He stopped drinking quite so much, began to bear down on his studies, and within a year was elected to Omega Psi, the national journalism fraternity; he became a member of the English Club; was invited to come with his cello, which he hadn't played in three years, and join in a student chamber-music group just forming; and he even ran successfully for secretary of the senior class. It was then that he met Marian Ross – a handsomely pale and slender girl who took a seat beside him in a Chaucer class.

Marian Ross wore her hair long and favored high-necked sweaters and always went around with a leather purse on a long strap swinging from her shoulder. Her eyes were large and seemed to take in everything at a glance. Ralph liked going out with Marian Ross. They went to The Keg and to a few other spots where everyone went, but they never let their going together or their subsequent engagement the next summer interfere with their studies. They were solemn students, and both sets of parents eventually gave approval to the match. Ralph and Marian did their student teaching at the same high school in Chico in the spring and went through graduation exercises together in June. They married in St James Episcopal Church two weeks later.

They had held hands the night before their wedding and pledged to preserve forever the excitement and the mystery of marriage.

★   ★   ★

For their honeymoon they drove to Guadalajara, and while they both enjoyed visiting the decayed churches and the poorly lighted museums and the afternoons they spent shopping and exploring in the marketplace, Ralph was secretly appalled by the squalor and open lust he saw and was anxious to return to the safety of California. But the one vision he would always remember and which disturbed him most of all had nothing to do with Mexico. It was late afternoon, almost evening, and Marian was leaning motionless on her arms over the ironwork balustrade of their rented *casita* as Ralph came up the dusty road below. Her hair was long and hung down in front over her shoulders, and she was looking away from him, staring at something in the distance. She wore a white blouse with a bright red scarf at her throat, and he could see her breasts pushing against the white cloth. He had a bottle of dark, unlabeled wine under his arm, and the whole incident put Ralph in mind of something from a film, an intensely dramatic moment into which Marian could be fitted but he could not.

Before they left for their honeymoon they had accepted positions at a high school in Eureka, a town in the lumbering region in the northern part of the state. After a year, when they were sure the school and the town were exactly what they wanted to settle down to, they made a payment on a house in the Fire Hill district. Ralph felt, without really thinking about it, that he and Marian understood each other perfectly – as well, at least, as any two people might. Moreover, Ralph felt he understood himself – what he could do, what he could not do, and where he was headed with the prudent measure of himself that he made.

Their two children, Dorothea and Robert, were now five and four years old. A few months after Robert was born, Marian was offered a post as a French and English instructor at the junior college at the edge of town, and Ralph had stayed on at the high school. They considered themselves a happy couple, with only a single injury to their marriage, and that was well in the past, two years ago this winter. It was something they had never talked about since. But Ralph thought about it sometimes – indeed, he was willing to admit he thought about it more and more. Increasingly, ghastly images would be projected on his eyes, certain unthinkable particularities. For he had taken it into his head that his wife had once betrayed him with a man named Mitchell Anderson.

But now it was a Sunday night in November and the children were asleep and Ralph was sleepy and he sat on the couch grading papers and could hear the radio playing softly in the kitchen, where Marian was ironing, and he felt enormously happy. He stared a while longer at the papers in front of him, then gathered them all up and turned off the lamp.

"Finished, love?" Marian said with a smile when he appeared in the doorway. She was sitting on a tall stool, and she stood the iron up on its end as if she had been waiting for him.

"Damn it, no," he said with an exaggerated grimace, tossing the papers on the kitchen table.

She laughed – bright, pleasant – and held up her face to be kissed, and he gave her a little peck on the cheek. He pulled out a chair from the table and sat down, leaned back on the legs and looked at her. She smiled again and then lowered her eyes.

"I'm already half asleep," he said.

"Coffee?" she said, reaching over and laying the back of her hand against the percolator.

He shook his head.

She took up the cigarette she had burning in the ashtray,

49

smoked it while she stared at the floor, and then put it back in the ashtray. She looked at him, and a warm expression moved across her face. She was tall and limber, with a good bust, narrow hips, and wide wonderful eyes.

"Do you ever think about that party?" she asked, still looking at him.

He was stunned and shifted in the chair, and he said, "Which party? You mean the one two or three years ago?"

She nodded.

He waited, and when she offered no further comment, he said, "What about it? Now that you brought it up, what about it?" Then: "He kissed you, after all, that night, didn't he? I mean, I knew he did. He did try to kiss you, or didn't he?"

"I was just thinking about it and I asked you, that's all," she said. "Sometimes I think about it," she said.

"Well, he did, didn't he? Come on, Marian," he said.

"Do you ever think about that night?" she said.

He said, "Not really. It was a long time ago, wasn't it? Three or four years ago. You can tell me now," he said. "This is still old Jackson you're talking to, remember?" And they both laughed abruptly together and abruptly she said, "Yes." She said, "He did kiss me a few times." She smiled.

He knew he should try to match her smile, but he could not. He said, "You told me before he didn't. You said he only put his arm around you while he was driving. So which is it?"

"What did you do that for?" she was saying dreamily. "Where were you all night?" he was screaming, standing over her, legs watery, fist drawn back to hit again. Then she said, "I didn't do anything. Why did you hit me?" she said.

"How did we ever get onto this?" she said.

"You brought it up," he said.

She shook her head. "I don't know what made me think

of it." She pulled in her upper lip and stared at the floor. Then she straightened her shoulders and looked up. "If you'll move this ironing board for me, love, I'll make us a hot drink. A buttered rum. How does that sound?"

"Good," he said.

She went into the living room and turned on the lamp and bent to pick up a magazine from the floor. He watched her hips under the plaid woolen skirt. She moved in front of the window and stood looking out at the streetlight. She smoothed her palm down over her skirt, then began tucking in her blouse. He wondered if she wondered if he were watching her.

After he stood the ironing board in its alcove on the porch, he sat down again and, when she came into the kitchen, he said, "Well, what else went on between you and Mitchell Anderson that night?"

"Nothing," she said. "I was thinking about something else."

"What?"

"About the children, the dress I want Dorothea to have for next Easter. And about the class I'm going to have tomorrow. I was thinking of seeing how they'd go for a little Rimbaud," and she laughed. "I didn't mean to rhyme – really, Ralph, and really, nothing else happened. I'm sorry I ever said anything about it."

"Okay," he said.

He stood up and leaned against the wall by the refrigerator and watched her as she spooned out sugar into two cups and then stirred in the rum. The water was beginning to boil.

"Look, honey, it *has* been brought up now," he said, "and it *was* four years ago, so there's no reason at all I can think of that we *can't* talk about it now if we *want* to. Is there?"

She said, "There's really nothing to talk about."

He said, "I'd like to know."

She said, "Know what?"

"Whatever else he did besides kiss you. We're adults. We haven't seen the Andersons in literally years and we'll probably never see them again and it happened a *long* time ago, so what reason could there possibly be that we can't talk about it?" He was a little surprised at the reasoning quality in his voice. He sat down and looked at the tablecloth and then looked up at her again. "Well?" he said.

"Well," she said, with an impish grin, tilting her head to one side girlishly, remembering. "No, Ralph, really. I'd really just rather not."

"For Christ's sake, Marian! *Now* I mean it," he said, and he suddenly understood that he did.

She turned off the gas under the water and put her hands out on the stool; then she sat down again, hooking her heels over the bottom step. She sat forward, resting her arms across her knees, her breasts pushing at her blouse. She picked at something on her skirt and then looked up.

"You remember Emily'd already gone home with the Beattys, and for some reason Mitchell had stayed on. He looked a little out of sorts that night, to begin with. I don't know, maybe they weren't getting along, Emily and him, but I don't know that. And there were you and I, the Franklins, and Mitchell Anderson still there. All of us a little drunk. I'm not sure how it happened, Ralph, but Mitchell and I just happened to find ourselves alone together in the kitchen for a minute, and there was no whiskey left, only a part of a bottle of that white wine we had. It must've been close to one o'clock, because Mitchell said, 'If we ride on giant wings we can make it before the liquor store closes.' You know how he could be so theatrical when he wanted? Soft-shoe stuff, facial expressions? Anyway, he was very witty about it all. At least it seemed that way at the time.

And very drunk, too, I might add. So was I, for that matter. It was an impulse, Ralph. I don't know why I did it, don't ask me, but when he said let's go – I agreed. We went out the back, where his car was parked. We went just as . . . we were . . . didn't even get our coats out of the closet, thought we'd just be gone a few minutes. I don't know what we thought, *I* thought, I don't know *why* I went, Ralph. It was an impulse, that's all I can say. It was the wrong impulse." She paused. "It was my fault that night, Ralph, and I'm sorry. I shouldn't have done anything like that – I *know* that."

"Christ!" The word leaped out of him. "But you've always been that way, Marian!" And he knew at once that he had uttered a new and profound truth.

His mind filled with a swarm of accusations, and he tried to focus on one in particular. He looked down at his hands and noticed they had the same lifeless feeling they had had when he had seen her on the balcony. He picked up the red grading pencil lying on the table and then he put it down again.

"I'm listening," he said.

"Listening to what?" she said. "You're swearing and getting upset, Ralph. For nothing – nothing, honey! . . . there's nothing *else*," she said.

"Go on," he said.

She said, "*What* is the matter with us, anyway? Do you know how this started? Because I don't know how this started."

He said, "Go on, Marian."

"That's *all*, Ralph," she said. "I've told you. We went for a ride. We talked. He kissed me. I still don't see how we could've been gone three hours – or whatever it was you said we were."

"Tell me, Marian," he said, and he knew there was more and knew he had always known. He felt a fluttering in his stomach, and then he said, "No. If you don't want to tell me, that's all right. Actually, I guess I'd just as soon leave it at that," he said. He thought fleetingly that he would be someplace else tonight doing something else, that it would be silent somewhere if he had not married.

"Ralph," she said, "you won't be angry, will you? Ralph? We're just talking. You won't, will you?" She had moved over to a chair at the table.

He said, "I won't."

She said, "Promise?"

He said, "Promise."

She lit a cigarette. He had suddenly a great desire to see the children, to get them up and out of bed, heavy and turning in their sleep, and to hold each of them on a knee, to jog them until they woke up. He moved all his attention into one of the tiny black coaches in the tablecloth. Four tiny white prancing horses pulled each one of the black coaches and the figure driving the horses had his arms up and wore a tall hat, and suitcases were strapped down atop the coach, and what looked like a kerosene lamp hung from the side, and if he were listening at all it was from inside the black coach.

". . . We went straight to the liquor store, and I waited in the car until he came out. He had a sack in one hand and one of those plastic bags of ice in the other. He weaved a little getting into the car. I hadn't realized he was so drunk until we started driving again. I noticed the way he was driving. It was terribly slow. He was all hunched over the wheel. His eyes staring. We were talking about a lot of things that didn't make sense. I can't remember. We were talking about Nietzsche. Strindberg. He was directing *Miss Julie* second semester. And then something about Norman Mailer stabbing his wife in the breast. And then he stopped for a minute in the middle of the road. And we each took a drink out of the bottle. He said he'd hate to think of me being stabbed in the breast. He said he'd like to kiss my breast. He drove the car off the road. He put his head on my lap. . . ."

She hurried on, and he sat with his hands folded on the table and watched her lips. His eyes skipped around the kitchen — stove, napkin-holder, stove, cupboards, toaster, back to her lips, back to the coach in the tablecloth. He felt a peculiar desire for her flicker through his groin, and then he felt the steady rocking of the coach and he wanted to call *stop* and then he heard her say, "He said shall we have a go at it?" And then she was saying, "I'm to blame. I'm the one to blame. He said he'd leave it all up to me, I could do whatever I want."

He shut his eyes. He shook his head, tried to create possibilities, other conclusions. He actually wondered if he could restore that night two years ago and imagined himself coming into the kitchen just as they were at the door, heard himself telling her in a hearty voice, oh no, no, you're not going out for anything with that Mitchell Anderson! The fellow is drunk and he's a bad driver to boot and you have to go to bed now and get up with little Robert and Dorothea in the morning and stop! Thou shalt stop!

He opened his eyes. She had a hand up over her face and was crying noisily.

"Why did you, Marian?" he asked.

She shook her head without looking up.

Then suddenly he knew! His mind buckled. For a minute he could only stare dumbly at his hands. He knew! His mind roared with the knowing.

"Christ! No! Marian! *Jesus Christ!*" he said, springing back from the table. "Christ! *No*, Marian!"

"No, no," she said, throwing her head back.

"You let him!" he screamed.

"No, no," she pleaded.

"You let him! A go at it! Didn't you? Didn't you? A *go* at it! Is that what he said? Answer me!" he screamed. "Did he come in you? Did you let him come in you when you were having your go at it?

"Listen, listen to me, Ralph," she whimpered, "I swear to you he didn't. He didn't come. He didn't come in me." She rocked from side to side in the chair.

"Oh God! God *damn* you!" he shrieked.

"God!" she said, getting up, holding out her hands, "Are we crazy, Ralph? Have we lost our minds? Ralph? Forgive me, Ralph. Forgive –"

"Don't touch me! Get away from me!" he screamed. He was screaming.

She began to pant in her fright. She tried to head him off. But he took her by the shoulder and pushed her out of the way.

"Forgive me, Ralph! *Please.* Ralph!" she screamed.

II

He had to stop and lean against a car before going on. Two couples in evening clothes were coming down the sidewalk toward him, and one of the men was telling a story in a loud voice. The others were already laughing. Ralph pushed off from the car and crossed the street. In a few minutes he came to Blake's, where he stopped some afternoons for a beer with Dick Koenig before picking up the children from nursery school.

It was dark inside. Candles flamed in long-necked bottles at the tables along one wall. Ralph glimpsed shadowy figures of men and women talking, their heads close together. One of the couples, near the door, stopped talking and looked up at him. A boxlike fixture in the ceiling revolved overhead, throwing out pins of light. Two men sat at the end of the bar, and a dark cutout of a man leaned over the jukebox in the corner, his hands splayed on each side of the glass. That man is going to play something, Ralph thought as if making a momentous discovery, and he stood in the center of the floor, watching the man.

"Ralph! Mr. Wyman, sir!"

He looked around. It was David Parks calling to him from behind the bar. Ralph walked over, leaned heavily against the bar before sliding onto a stool.

"Should I draw one, Mr. Wyman?" Parks held a glass in his hand, smiling. Ralph nodded, watched Parks fill the glass, watched Parks hold the glass at an angle under the tap, smoothly straighten the glass as it filled.

"How's it going, Mr. Wyman?" Parks put his foot up on a shelf under the bar. "Who's going to win the game next week, Mr. Wyman?" Ralph shook his head, brought the beer to his lips. Parks coughed faintly. "I'll buy you one, Mr. Wyman. This one's on me." He put his leg down, nodded assurance, and reached under his apron into his pocket. "Here. I have it right here," Ralph said and pulled out some change, examined it in his hand. A quarter, nickel, two dimes, two pennies. He counted as if there were a code to be uncovered. He laid down the quarter and stood up, pushing the change back into his pocket. The man was still in front of the jukebox, his hands still out to its sides.

Outside, Ralph turned around, trying to decide what to do. His heart was jumping as if he'd been running. The door opened behind him and a man and woman came out. Ralph stepped out of the way and they got into a car parked at the curb and Ralph saw the woman toss her hair as she got into the car: He had never seen anything so frightening.

He walked to the end of the block, crossed the street, and

walked another block before he decided to head downtown. He walked hurriedly, his hands balled into his pockets, his shoes smacking the pavement. He kept blinking his eyes and thought it incredible that this was where he lived. He shook his head. He would have liked to sit someplace for a while and think about it, but he knew he could not sit, could not think about it. He remembered a man he saw once sitting on a curb in Arcata, an old man with a growth of beard and a brown wool cap who just sat there with his arms between his legs. And then Ralph thought: Marian! Dorothea! Robert! It was impossible. He tried to imagine how all this would seem twenty years from now. But he could not imagine anything. And then he imagined snatching up a note being passed among his students and it said *Shall we have a go at it?* Then he could not think. Then he felt profoundly indifferent. Then he thought of Marian. He thought of Marian as he had seen her a little while ago, face crumpled. Then Marian on the floor, blood on her teeth: "Why did you hit me?" Then Marian reaching under her dress to unfasten her garter belt! Then Marian lifting her dress as she arched back! Then Marian ablaze, Marian crying out, *Go! Go! Go!*

He stopped. He believed he was going to vomit. He moved to the curb. He kept swallowing, looked up as a car of yelling teenagers went by and gave him a long blast on their musical horn. Yes, there was a great evil pushing at the world, he thought, and it only needed a little slipway, a little opening.

He came to Second Street, the part of town people called "Two Street." It started here at Shelton, under the streetlight where the old roominghouses ended, and ran for four or five blocks on down to the pier, where fishing boats tied up. He had been down here once, six years ago, to a secondhand shop to finger through the dusty shelves of old books. There was a liquor store across the street, and he could see a man standing just inside the glass door, looking at a newspaper.

A bell over the door tinkled. Ralph almost wept from the sound of it. He bought some cigarettes and went out again, continuing along the street, looking in windows, some with signs taped up: a dance, the Shrine circus that had come and gone last summer, an election – *Fred C. Walters for Councilman.* One of the windows he looked through had sinks and pipe joints scattered around on a table, and this too brought tears to his eyes. He came to a Vic Tanney gym where he could see light sneaking under the curtains pulled across a big window and could hear water splashing in the pool inside and the echo of exhilarated voices calling across water. There was more light now, coming from bars and cafés on both sides of the street, and more people, groups of three or four, but now and then a man by himself or a woman in bright slacks walking rapidly. He stopped in front of a window and watched some Negroes shooting pool, smoke drifting in the light burning above the table. One of the men, chalking his cue, hat on, cigarette in his mouth, said something to another man and both men grinned, and then the first man looked intently at the balls and lowered himself over the table.

Ralph stopped in front of Jim's Oyster House. He had never been here before, had never been to any of these places before. Above the door the name was spelled out in yellow lightbulbs: JIM'S OYSTER HOUSE. Above this, fixed to an iron grill, there was a huge neon-lighted clam shell with a man's legs sticking out. The torso was hidden in the shell and the legs flashed red, on and off, up and down, so that they seemed to be kicking. Ralph lit another cigarette from the one he had and pushed the door open.

It was crowded, people bunched on the dance floor, their arms laced around each other, waiting in positions for the band to begin again. Ralph pushed his way to the bar, and once a drunken woman took hold of his coat. There were no stools and he had to stand at the end of the bar between a Coast Guardsman and a shriveled man in denims. In the mirror he could see the men in the band getting up from the table where they had been sitting. They wore white shirts and dark slacks with little red string ties around their necks. There was a fireplace with gas flames behind a stack of metal logs, and the band platform was to the side of this. One of the musicians plucked the strings of his electric guitar, said something to the others with a knowing grin. The band began to play.

Ralph raised his glass and drained it. Down the bar he could hear a woman say angrily, "Well, there's going to be trouble, that's all I've got to say." The musicians came to the end of their number and started another. One of the men, the bass player, moved to the microphone and began to sing. But Ralph could not understand the words. When the band took another break, Ralph looked around for the toilet. He could make out doors opening and closing at the far end of the bar and headed in that direction. He staggered a little and knew he was drunk now. Over one of the doors was a rack of antlers. He saw a man go in and he saw another man catch the door and come out. Inside, in line behind three other men, he found himself staring at opened thighs and vulva drawn on the wall over a pocket-comb machine. Beneath was scrawled EAT ME, and lower down someone had added *Betty M. Eats It—RA 52275*. The man ahead moved up, and Ralph took a step forward, his heart squeezed in the weight of Betty. Finally, he moved to the bowl and urinated. It was a bolt of lightning cracking. He sighed, leaned forward, and let his head rest against the wall. Oh, Betty, he thought. His life had changed, he was willing to understand. Were there other men, he wondered drunkenly, who could look at one event in their lives and perceive in it the tiny makings of the catastrophe that thereafter set their lives on a different course? He stood there a while longer, and then he looked down: he had urinated on his fingers. He moved to the wash basin, ran water over his hands after deciding against the dirty bar of soap. As he was unrolling the towel, he put his face up close to the pitted mirror and looked into his eyes. A face: nothing out of the ordinary. He touched the glass, and then he moved away as a man tried to get past him to the sink.

When he came out the door, he noticed another door at the other end of the corridor. He went to it and looked through the glass panel in the door at four card players around a green felt table. It seemed to Ralph immensely still and restful inside, the silent movements of the men languorous and heavy with meaning. He leaned against the glass and watched until he felt the men watching him.

Back at the bar there was a flourish of guitars and people began whistling and clapping. A fat middle-aged woman in a white evening dress was being helped onto the platform. She kept trying to pull back but Ralph could see that it was a mock effort, and finally she accepted the mike and made a little curtsy. The people whistled and stamped their feet. Suddenly he knew that nothing could save him but to be in the same room with the card players, watching. He took out his wallet, keeping his hands up over the sides as he looked to see how much he had. Behind him the woman began to sing in a low drowsy voice.

The man dealing looked up.

"Decided to join us?" he said, sweeping Ralph with his eyes and checking the table again. The others raised their eyes for an instant and then looked back at the cards skimming around the table. The men picked up their cards, and the man sitting with his back to Ralph breathed impressively out his nose, turned around in his chair and glared.

"Benny, bring another chair!" the dealer called to an old man sweeping under a table that had chairs turned up on the top. The dealer was a large man; he wore a white shirt, open at the collar, the sleeves rolled back once to expose forearms thick with black curling hair. Ralph drew a long breath.

"Want anything to drink?" Benny asked, carrying a chair to the table.

Ralph gave the old man a dollar and pulled out of his coat. The old man took the coat and hung it up by the door as he went out. Two of the men moved their chairs and Ralph sat down across from the dealer.

"How's it going?" the dealer said to Ralph, not looking up.

"All right," Ralph said.

The dealer said gently, still not looking up, "Low ball or five card. Table stakes, five-dollar limit on raises."

Ralph nodded, and when the hand was finished he bought fifteen dollars' worth of chips. He watched the cards as they flashed around the table, picked up his as he had seen his father do, sliding one card under the corner of another as each card fell in front of him. He raised his eyes once and looked at the faces of the others. He wondered if it had ever happened to any of them.

In half an hour he had won two hands, and, without counting the small pile of chips in front of him, he thought he must still have fifteen or even twenty dollars. He paid for another drink with a chip and was suddenly aware that he had come a long way that evening, a long way in his life. *Jackson*, he thought. He could be Jackson.

"You in or out?" one man asked. "Clyde, what's the bid, for Christ's sake?" the man said to the dealer.

"Three dollars," the dealer said.

"In," Ralph said. "I'm in." He put three chips into the pot.

The dealer looked up and then back at his cards. "You really want some action, we can go to my place when we finish here," the dealer said.

"No, that's all right," Ralph said. "Enough action tonight. I just found out tonight. My wife played around with another guy two years ago. I found out tonight." He cleared his throat.

One man laid down his cards and lit his cigar. He stared at Ralph as he puffed, then shook out the match and picked up his cards again. The dealer looked up, resting his open hands on the table, the black hair very crisp on his dark hands.

"You work here in town?" he said to Ralph.

"I live here," Ralph said. He felt drained, splendidly empty.

"We playing or not?" a man said. "Clyde?"

"Hold your water," the dealer said.

"For Christ's sake," the man said quietly.

"What did you find out tonight?" the dealer said.

"My wife," Ralph said. "I found out."

In the alley, he took out his wallet again, let his fingers number the bills he had left: two dollars – and he thought there was some change in his pocket. Enough for something to eat. But he was not hungry, and he sagged against the building trying to think. A car turned into the alley, stopped, backed out again. He started walking. He went the way he'd come. He stayed close to the buildings, out of the path of the loud groups of men and women streaming up and down the sidewalk. He heard a woman in a long coat say to the

63

man she was with, "It isn't that way at all, Bruce. You don't understand."

He stopped when he came to the liquor store. Inside he moved up to the counter and studied the long orderly rows of bottles. He bought a half pint of rum and some more cigarettes. The palm trees on the label of the bottle, the large drooping fronds with the lagoon in the background, had caught his eye, and then he realized *rum!* And he thought he would faint. The clerk, a thin bald man wearing suspenders, put the bottle in a paper sack and rang up the sale and winked. "Got you a little something tonight?" he said.

Outside, Ralph started toward the pier; he thought he'd like to see the water with the lights reflected on it. He thought how Dr. Maxwell would handle a thing like this, and he reached into the sack as he walked, broke the seal on the little bottle and stopped in a doorway to take a long drink and thought Dr. Maxwell would sit handsomely at the water's edge. He crossed some old streetcar tracks and turned onto another, darker street. He could already hear the waves splashing under the pier, and then he heard someone move up behind him. A small Negro in a leather jacket stepped out in front of him and said, "Just a minute there, man." Ralph tried to move around. The man said, "Christ, baby, that's my feet you're steppin on!" Before Ralph could run the Negro hit him hard in the stomach, and when Ralph groaned and tried to fall, the man hit him in the nose with his open hand, knocking him back against the wall, where he sat down with one leg turned under him and was learning how to raise himself up when the Negro slapped him on the cheek and knocked him sprawling onto the pavement.

III

He kept his eyes fixed in one place and saw them, dozens of them, wheeling and darting just under the overcast, seabirds, birds that came in off the ocean this time of morning. The street was black with the mist that was still falling, and he had to be careful not to step on the snails that trailed across the wet sidewalk. A car with its lights on slowed as it went past. Another car passed. Then another. He looked: mill workers, he whispered to himself. It was Monday morning. He turned a corner, walked past Blake's: blinds pulled, empty bottles standing like sentinels beside the door. It was cold. He walked as fast as he could, crossing his arms now and then and rubbing his shoulders. He came at last to his house, porch light on, windows dark. He crossed the lawn and went around to the back. He turned the knob, and the door opened quietly and the house was quiet. There was the tall stool beside the draining board. There was the table where they had sat. He had gotten up from the couch, come into the kitchen, sat down. What more had he done? He had done nothing more. He looked at the clock over the stove. He could see into the dining room, the table with the lace cloth, the heavy glass centerpiece of red flamingos, their wings opened, the draperies beyond the table open. Had she stood at that window watching for him? He stepped onto the living-room carpet. Her coat was thrown over the couch, and in the pale light he could make out a large ashtray full of her cork cigarette ends. He noticed the phone directory open on the coffee table as he went by. He stopped at the partially open door to their bedroom. Everything seemed to him open. For an instant he resisted the wish to look in at her, and then with his finger he pushed the door open a little bit more. She was sleeping, her head off the pillow, turned toward the wall, her hair black against the sheet, the covers bunched around her shoulders, covers pulled up from the foot of the bed. She was on her side, her secret body angled at the hips. He stared. What, after all, should he do? Take his things and leave? Go to a hotel? Make certain arrangements? How should a man act, given these circumstances? He understood things had been done. He did not understand what things now were to be done. The house was very quiet.

In the kitchen he let his head down onto his arms as he sat at the table. He did not know what to do. Not just now, he thought, not just in this, not just about this, today and tomorrow, but every day on earth. Then he heard the children stirring. He sat up and tried to smile as they came into the kitchen.

"Daddy, Daddy," they said, running to him with their little bodies.

"Tell us a story, Daddy," his son said, getting onto his lap.

"He can't tell us a story," his daughter said. "It's too early for a story. Isn't it, Daddy?"

"What's that on your face, Daddy?" his son said, pointing.

"Let me see!" his daughter said. "Let me see, Daddy."

"Poor Daddy," his son said.

"What did you do to your face, Daddy?" his daughter said.

"It's nothing," Ralph said. "It's all right, sweetheart. Now get down now, Robert, I hear your mother."

Ralph stepped quickly into the bathroom and locked the door.

"Is your father here?" he heard Marian calling. "Where is he, in the bathroom? Ralph?"

"Mama, Mama!" his daughter cried. "Daddy's face is hurt!"

"Ralph!" She turned the knob. "Ralph, let me in, please, darling. Ralph? Please let me in, darling. I want to see you. Ralph? Please!"

He said, "Go away, Marian."

She said, "I can't go away. Please, Ralph, open the door for a minute, darling. I just want to see you. Ralph. Ralph? The children said you were hurt. What's wrong, darling? Ralph?"

He said, "Go away."

She said, "Ralph, open up, please."

He said, "Will you please be quiet, please?"

He heard her waiting at the door, he saw the knob turn again, and then he could hear her moving around the kitchen, getting the children breakfast, trying to answer their questions. He looked at himself in the mirror a long time. He made faces at himself. He tried many expressions. Then he gave it up. He turned away from the mirror and sat down on the edge of the bathtub, began unlacing his shoes. He sat there with a shoe in his hand and looked at the clipper ships making their way across the wide blue sea of the plastic shower curtain. He thought of the little black coaches in the tablecloth and almost cried out *Stop!* He unbuttoned his shirt, leaned over the bathtub with a sigh, and pressed the plug into the drain. He ran hot water, and presently steam rose.

He stood naked on the tiles before getting into the water. He gathered in his fingers the slack flesh over his ribs. He studied his face again in the clouded mirror. He started in fear when Marian called his name.

"Ralph. The children are in their room playing. I called Von Williams and said you wouldn't be in today, and I'm going to stay home." Then she said, "I have a nice breakfast on the stove for you, darling, when you're through with your bath. Ralph?"

"Just be quiet, please," he said.

He stayed in the bathroom until he heard her in the children's room. She was dressing them, asking didn't they want to play with Warren and Roy? He went through the house and into the bedroom, where he shut the door. He looked at the bed before he crawled in. He lay on his back and stared at the ceiling. He had gotten up from the couch, had come into the kitchen, had . . . *sat* . . . *down*. He snapped shut his eyes and turned onto his side as Marian came into the room. She took off her robe and sat down on the bed. She put her hand under the covers and began stroking the lower part of his back.

"Ralph," she said.

He tensed at her fingers, and then he let go a little. It was easier to let go a little. Her hand moved over his hip and over his stomach and she was pressing her body over his now and moving over him and back and forth over him. He held himself, he later considered, as long as he could. And then he turned to her. He turned and turned in what might have been a stupendous sleep, and he was still turning, marveling at the impossible changes he felt moving over him.

So Much Water So Close to Home

MY HUSBAND EATS WITH good appetite but he seems tired, edgy. He chews slowly, arms on the table, and stares at something across the room. He looks at me and looks away again. He wipes his mouth on the napkin. He shrugs and goes on eating. Something has come between us though he would like me to believe otherwise.

"What are you staring at me for?" he asks. "What is it?" he says and puts his fork down.

"Was I staring?" I say and shake my head stupidly, stupidly.

The telephone rings. "Don't answer it," he says.

"It might be your mother," I say. "Dean – it might be something about Dean."

"Watch and see," he says.

I pick up the receiver and listen for a minute. He stops eating. I bite my lip and hang up.

"What did I tell you?" he says. He starts to eat again, then throws the napkin onto his plate. "Goddamn it, why can't people mind their own business? Tell me what I did wrong and I'll listen! It's not fair. She was dead, wasn't she? There were other men there besides me. We talked it over and we all decided. We'd only just got there. We'd walked for hours. We couldn't just turn around, we were five miles from the car. It was opening day. What the hell, I don't see anything wrong. No, I don't. And don't look at me that way, do you hear? I won't have you passing judgment on me. Not you."

"You know," I say and shake my head.

"What do I know, Claire? Tell me. Tell me what I know. I don't know anything except one thing: you hadn't better get worked up over this." He gives me what he thinks is a *meaningful* look. "She was dead, dead, dead, do you hear?" he says after a minute. "It's a damn shame, I agree. She was a young girl and it's a shame, and I'm sorry, as sorry as anyone else, but she was dead, Claire, dead. Now let's leave it alone. Please, Claire. Let's leave it alone now."

"That's the point," I say. "She was dead. But don't you see? She needed help."

"I give up," he says and raises his hands. He pushes his chair away from the table, takes his cigarettes and goes out to the patio with a can of beer. He walks back and forth for a minute and then sits in a lawn chair and picks up the paper once more. His name is there on the first page along with the names of his friends, the other men who made the "grisly find."

I close my eyes for a minute and hold onto the drainboard. I must not dwell on this any longer. I must get over it, put it out of sight, out of mind, etc., and "go on." I open my eyes. Despite everything, knowing all that may be in store, I rake my arm across the drainboard and send the dishes and glasses smashing and scattering across the floor.

He doesn't move. I know he has heard, he raises his head as if listening, but he doesn't move otherwise, doesn't turn around to look. I hate him for that, for not moving. He waits a minute, then draws on his cigarette and leans back in the chair. I pity him for listening, detached, and then settling back and drawing on his cigarette. The wind takes the smoke out of his mouth in a thin stream. Why do I notice that? He can never know how much I pity him for that, for sitting still and listening, and letting the smoke stream out of his mouth. . . .

He planned his fishing trip into the mountains last Sunday, a week before the Memorial Day weekend. He and Gordon Johnson, Mel Dorn, Vern Williams. They play poker, bowl, and fish together. They fish together every spring and early summer, the first two or three months of the season, before family vacations, little league baseball, and visiting relatives can intrude. They are decent men, family men, responsible at their jobs. They have sons and daughters who go to school with our son, Dean. On Friday afternoon these four men left for a three-day fishing trip to the Naches River. They parked the car in the mountains and hiked several miles to where they wanted to fish. They carried their bedrolls, food and cooking utensils, their playing cards, their whiskey. The first evening at the river, even before they could set up camp, Mel Dorn found the girl floating face down in the river, nude, lodged near the shore in some branches. He called the other men and they all came to look at her. They talked about what to do. One of the men – Stuart didn't say which – perhaps it was Vern Williams, he is a heavy-set, easy man who laughs often – one of them thought they should start back to the car at once. The others stirred the sand with their shoes and said they felt inclined to stay. They pleaded fatigue, the late hour, the fact that the girl "wasn't going anywhere." In the end they all decided to stay. They went ahead and set up the camp and built a fire and drank their whiskey. They drank a lot of whiskey and when the moon came up they talked about the girl. Someone thought they should do something to prevent the body from floating away. Somehow they thought that this might create a problem for them if it floated away during the night. They took flashlights and stumbled down to the river. The wind was up, a cold wind, and waves from the river lapped the sandy bank. One of the

men, I don't know who, it might have been Stuart, he could
have done it, waded into the water and took the girl by the
fingers and pulled her, still face down, closer to shore, into
shallow water, and then took a piece of nylon cord and tied
it around her wrist and then secured the cord to tree roots,
all the while the flashlights of the other men played over the
girl's body. Afterward, they went back to camp and drank
more whiskey. Then they went to sleep. The next morning,
Saturday, they cooked breakfast, drank lots of coffee, more
whiskey, and then split up to fish, two men upriver, two
men down.

That night, after they had cooked their fish and potatoes
and had more coffee and whiskey, they took their dishes
down to the river and rinsed them off a few yards from
where the body lay in the water. They drank again and then
they took out their cards and played and drank until they
couldn't see the cards any longer. Vern Williams went to
sleep, but the others told coarse stories and spoke of vulgar
or dishonest escapades out of their past, and no one men-
tioned the girl until Gordon Johnson, who'd forgotten for a
minute, commented on the firmness of the trout they'd
caught, and the terrible coldness of the river water. They
stopped talking then but continued to drink until one of them
tripped and fell cursing against the lantern, and then they
climbed into their sleeping bags.

The next morning they got up late, drank more whiskey,
fished a little as they kept drinking whiskey. Then, at one
o'clock in the afternoon, Sunday, a day earlier than they'd
planned, they decided to leave. They took down their tents,
rolled their sleeping bags, gathered their pans, pots, fish, and
fishing gear, and hiked out. They didn't look at the girl again
before they left. When they reached the car they drove the
highway in silence until they came to a telephone. Stuart
made the call to the sheriff's office while the others stood

around in the hot sun and listened. He gave the man on the other end of the line all of their names – they had nothing to hide, they weren't ashamed of anything – and agreed to wait at the service station until someone could come for more detailed directions and individual statements.

He came home at eleven o'clock that night. I was asleep but woke when I heard him in the kitchen. I found him leaning against the refrigerator drinking a can of beer. He put his heavy arms around me and rubbed his hands up and down my back, the same hands he'd left with two days before, I thought.

In bed he put his hands on me again and then waited, as if thinking of something else. I turned slightly and then moved my legs. Afterward, I know he stayed awake for a long time, for he was awake when I fell asleep; and later, when I stirred for a minute, opening my eyes at a slight noise, a rustle of sheets, it was almost daylight outside, birds were singing, and he was on his back smoking and looking at the curtained window. Half-asleep I said his name, but he didn't answer. I fell asleep again.

He was up this morning before I could get out of bed – to see if there was anything about it in the paper, I suppose. The telephone began to ring shortly after eight o'clock.

"Go to hell," I heard him shout into the receiver. The telephone rang again a minute later, and I hurried into the kitchen. "I have nothing else to add to what I've already said to the sheriff. That's right!" He slammed down the receiver.

"What is going on?" I said, alarmed.

"Sit down," he said slowly. His fingers scraped, scraped against his stubble of whiskers. "I have to tell you something. Something happened while we were fishing." We sat across from each other at the table, and then he told me.

I drank coffee and stared at him as he spoke. Then I read the account in the newspaper that he shoved across the table:

". . . unidentified girl eighteen to twenty-four years of age . . . body three to five days in the water . . . rape a possible motive . . . preliminary results show death by strangulation . . . cuts and bruises on her breasts and pelvic area . . . autopsy . . . rape, pending further investigation."

"You've got to understand," he said. "Don't look at me like that. Be careful now, I mean it. Take it easy, Claire."

"Why didn't you tell me last night?" I asked.

"I just . . . didn't. What do you mean?" he said.

"You know what I mean," I said. I looked at his hands, the broad fingers, knuckles covered with hair, moving, lighting a cigarette now, fingers that had moved over me, into me last night.

He shrugged. "What difference does it make, last night, this morning? It was late. You were sleepy, I thought I'd wait until this morning to tell you." He looked out to the patio: a robin flew from the lawn to the picnic table and preened its feathers.

"It isn't true," I said. "You didn't leave her there like that?"

He turned quickly and said, "What'd I do? Listen to me carefully now, once and for all. Nothing happened. I have nothing to be sorry for or feel guilty about. Do you hear me?"

I got up from the table and went to Dean's room. He was awake and in his pajamas, putting together a puzzle. I helped him find his clothes and then went back to the kitchen and put his breakfast on the table. The telephone rang two or three more times and each time Stuart was abrupt while he talked and angry when he hung up. He called Mel Dorn and Gordon Johnson and spoke with them, slowly, seriously, and then he opened a beer and smoked a cigarette while Dean ate, asked him about school, his friends, etc., exactly as if nothing had happened.

Dean wanted to know what he'd done while he was gone, and Stuart took some fish out of the freezer to show him.

"I'm taking him to your mother's for the day," I said.

"Sure," Stuart said and looked at Dean who was holding one of the frozen trout. "If you want to and he wants to, that is. You don't have to, you know. There's nothing wrong."

"I'd like to anyway," I said.

"Can I go swimming there?" Dean asked and wiped his fingers on his pants.

"I believe so," I said. "It's a warm day so take your suit, and I'm sure your grandmother will say it's okay."

Stuart lighted a cigarette and looked at us.

Dean and I drove across town to Stuart's mother's. She lives in an apartment building with a pool and a sauna bath. Her name is Catherine Kane. Her name, Kane, is the same as mine, which seems impossible. Years ago, Stuart has told me, she used to be called Candy by her friends. She is a tall, cold woman with white-blonde hair. She gives me the feeling that she is always judging, judging. I explain briefly in a low voice what has happened (she hasn't yet read the newspaper) and promise to pick Dean up that evening. "He brought his swimming suit," I say. "Stuart and I have to talk about some things," I add vaguely. She looks at me steadily from over her glasses. Then she nods and turns to Dean, saying "How are you, my little man?" She stoops and puts her arms around him. She looks at me again as I open the door to leave. She has a way of looking at me without saying anything.

When I return home Stuart is eating something at the table and drinking beer. . . .

After a time I sweep up the broken dishes and glassware and go outside. Stuart is lying on his back on the grass now, the newspaper and can of beer within reach, staring at the sky. It's breezy but warm out and birds call.

"Stuart, could we go for a drive?" I say. "Anywhere."

He rolls over and looks at me and nods. "We'll pick up some beer," he says. "I hope you're feeling better about this. Try to understand, that's all I ask." He gets to his feet and touches me on the hip as he goes past. "Give me a minute and I'll be ready."

We drive through town without speaking. Before we reach the country he stops at a roadside market for beer. I notice a great stack of papers just inside the door. On the top step a fat woman in a print dress holds out a licorice stick to a little girl. In a few minutes we cross Everson Creek and turn into a picnic area a few feet from the water. The creek flows under the bridge and into a large pond a few hundred yards away. There are a dozen or so men and boys scattered around the banks of the pond under the willows, fishing.

So much water so close to home, why did he have to go miles away to fish?

"Why did you have to go there of all places?" I say.

"The Naches? We always go there. Every year, at least once." We sit on a bench in the sun and he opens two cans of beer and gives one to me. "How the hell was I to know anything like that would happen?" He shakes his head and shrugs, as if it had all happened years ago, or to someone else. "Enjoy the afternoon, Claire. Look at this weather."

"They said they were innocent."

"Who? What are you talking about?"

"The Maddox brothers. They killed a girl named Arlene Hubly near the town where I grew up, and then cut off her head and threw her into the Cle Elum River. She and I went to the same high school. It happened when I was a girl."

"What a hell of a thing to be thinking about," he says. "Come on, get off it. You're going to get me riled in a minute. How about it now? Claire?"

I look at the creek. I float toward the pond, eyes open, face down, staring at the rocks and moss on the creek bottom until I am carried into the lake where I am pushed by the breeze. Nothing will be any different. We will go on and on and on and on. We will go on even now, as if nothing had happened. I look at him across the picnic table with such intensity that his face drains.

"I don't know what's wrong with you," he says. "I don't –"

I slap him before I realize. I raise my hand, wait a fraction of a second, and then slap his cheek hard. This is crazy, I think as I slap him. We need to lock our fingers together. We need to help one another. This is crazy.

He catches my wrist before I can strike again and raises his own hand. I crouch, waiting, and see something come into his eyes and then dart away. He drops his hand. I drift even faster around and around in the pond.

"Come on, get in the car," he says. "I'm taking you home."

"No, no," I say, pulling back from him.

"Come on," he says. "Goddamn it."

"You're not being fair to me," he says later in the car. Fields and trees and farmhouses fly by outside the window. "You're not being fair. To either one of us. Or to Dean, I might add. Think about Dean for a minute. Think about me. Think about someone else besides your goddamn self for a change."

There is nothing I can say to him now. He tries to concentrate on the road, but he keeps looking into the rearview mirror. Out of the corner of his eye, he looks across the seat to where I sit with my knees drawn up under my chin. The sun blazes against my arm and the side of my face. He opens another beer while he drives, drinks from it, then shoves the can between his legs and lets out breath. He knows. I could laugh in his face. I could weep.

★　　★　　★

Stuart believes he is letting me sleep this morning. But I was awake long before the alarm sounded, thinking, lying on the far side of the bed, away from his hairy legs and his thick, sleeping fingers. He gets Dean off for school, and then he shaves, dresses, and leaves for work. Twice he looks into the bedroom and clears his throat, but I keep my eyes closed.

In the kitchen I find a note from him signed "Love." I sit in the breakfast nook in the sunlight and drink coffee and make a coffee ring on the note. The telephone has stopped ringing, that's something. No more calls since last night. I look at the paper and turn it this way and that on the table. Then I pull it close and read what it says. The body is still unidentified, unclaimed, apparently unmissed. But for the last twenty-four hours men have been examining it, putting things into it, cutting, weighing, measuring, putting back again, sewing up, looking for the exact cause and moment of death. Looking for evidence of rape. I'm sure they hope for rape. Rape would make it easier to understand. The paper says the body will be taken to Keith & Keith Funeral Home pending arrangements. People are asked to come forward with information, etc.

Two things are certain: 1) people no longer care what happens to other people; and 2) nothing makes any real difference any longer. Look at what has happened. Yet nothing will change for Stuart and me. Really change, I mean. We will grow older, both of us, you can see it in our faces already, in the bathroom mirror, for instance, mornings when we use the bathroom at the same time. And certain things around us will change, become easier or harder, one thing or the other, but nothing will ever really be any different. I believe that. We have made our decisions, our lives have been set in motion, and they will go on and on until they stop. But if that is true, then what? I mean, what if you believe that, but

you keep it covered up, until one day something happens
that should change something, but then you see nothing is
going to change after all. What then? Meanwhile, the people
around you continue to talk and act as if you were the same
person as yesterday, or last night, or five minutes before,
but you are really undergoing a crisis, your heart feels
damaged. . . .

The past is unclear. It's as if there is a film over those
early years. I can't even be sure that the things I remember
happening really happened to me. There was a girl who had
a mother and father – the father ran a small café where the
mother acted as waitress and cashier – who moved as if in a
dream through grade school and high school and then, in a
year or two, into secretarial school. Later, much later – what
happened to the time in between? – she is in another town
working as a receptionist for an electronics parts firm and
becomes acquainted with one of the engineers who asks her
for a date. Eventually, seeing that's his aim, she lets him
seduce her. She had an intuition at the time, an insight about
the seduction that later, try as she might, she couldn't recall.
After a short while they decide to get married, but already
the past, her past, is slipping away. The future is something
she can't imagine. She smiles, as if she has a secret, when
she thinks about the future. Once, during a particularly bad
argument, over what she can't now remember, five years or
so after they were married, he tells her that someday this
affair (his words: "this affair") will end in violence. She
remembers this. She files this away somewhere and begins
repeating it aloud from time to time. Sometimes she spends
the whole morning on her knees in the sandbox behind the
garage playing with Dean and one or two of his friends. But
every afternoon at four o'clock her head begins to hurt. She
holds her forehead and feels dizzy with the pain. Stuart asks
her to see a doctor and she does, secretly pleased at the doc-

tor's solicitous attention. She goes away for a while to a place the doctor recommends. Stuart's mother comes out from Ohio in a hurry to care for the child. But she, Claire, spoils everything and returns home in a few weeks. His mother moves out of the house and takes an apartment across town and perches there, as if waiting. One night in bed when they are both near sleep, Claire tells him that she heard some women patients at the clinic discussing fellatio. She thinks this is something he might like to hear. Stuart is pleased at hearing this. He strokes her arm. Things are going to be okay, he says. From now on everything is going to be different and better for them. He has received a promotion and a substantial raise. They've even bought another car, a station wagon, her car. They're going to live in the here and now. He says he feels able to relax for the first time in years. In the dark, he goes on stroking her arm. . . . He continues to bowl and play cards regularly. He goes fishing with three friends of his.

That evening three things happen: Dean says that the children at school told him that his father found a dead body in the river. He wants to know about it.

Stuart explains quickly, leaving out most of the story, saying only that, yes, he and three other men did find a body while they were fishing.

"What kind of body?" Dean asks. "Was it a girl?"

"Yes, it was a girl. A woman. Then we called the sheriff." Stuart looks at me.

"What'd he say?" Dean asks.

"He said he'd take care of it."

"What did it look like? Was it scary?"

"That's enough talk," I say. "Rinse your plate, Dean, and then you're excused."

"But what'd it look like?" he persists. "I want to know."

"You heard me," I say. "Did you hear me, Dean? Dean!" I want to shake him. I want to shake him until he cries.

"Do what your mother says," Stuart tells him quietly. "It was just a body, and that's all there is to it."

I am clearing the table when Stuart comes up behind and touches my arm. His fingers burn. I start, almost losing a plate.

"What's the matter with you?" he says, dropping his hand. "Claire, what is it?"

"You scared me," I say.

"That's what I mean. I should be able to touch you without you jumping out of your skin." He stands in front of me with a little grin, trying to catch my eyes, and then he puts his arm around my waist. With his other hand he takes my free hand and puts it on the front of his pants.

"Please, Stuart." I pull away and he steps back and snaps his fingers.

"Hell with it then," he says. "Be that way if you want. But just remember."

"Remember what?" I say quickly. I look at him and hold my breath.

He shrugs. "Nothing, nothing," he says.

The second thing that happens is that while we are watching television that evening, he in his leather recliner chair, I on the sofa with a blanket and magazine, the house quiet except for the television, a voice cuts into the program to say that the murdered girl has been identified. Full details will follow on the eleven o'clock news.

We look at each other. In a few minutes he gets up and says he is going to fix a nightcap. Do I want one?

"No," I say.

"I don't mind drinking alone," he says. "I thought I'd ask."

I can see he is obscurely hurt, and I look away, ashamed and yet angry at the same time.

He stays in the kitchen a long while, but comes back with his drink just when the news begins.

First the announcer repeats the story of the four local fishermen finding the body. Then the station shows a high school graduation photograph of the girl, a dark-haired girl with a round face and full, smiling lips. There's a film of the girl's parents entering the funeral home to make the identification. Bewildered, sad, they shuffle slowly up the sidewalk to the front steps to where a man in a dark suit stands waiting, holding the door. Then, it seems as if only seconds have passed, as if they have merely gone inside the door and turned around and come out again, the same couple is shown leaving the building, the woman in tears, covering her face with a handkerchief, the man stopping long enough to say to a reporter, "It's her, it's Susan. I can't say anything right now. I hope they get the person or persons who did it before it happens again. This violence. . . ." He motions feebly at the television camera. Then the man and woman get into an old car and drive away into the late afternoon traffic.

The announcer goes on to say that the girl, Susan Miller, had gotten off work as a cashier in a movie theater in Summit, a town 120 miles north of our town. A green, late-model car pulled up in front of the theater and the girl, who according to witnesses looked as if she'd been waiting, went over to the car and got in, leading the authorities to suspect that the driver of the car was a friend, or at least an acquaintance. The authorities would like to talk to the driver of the green car.

Stuart clears his throat, then leans back in the chair and sips his drink.

The third thing that happens is that after the news Stuart

stretches, yawns, and looks at me. I get up and begin making a bed for myself on the sofa.

"What are you doing?" he says, puzzled.

"I'm not sleepy," I say, avoiding his eyes. "I think I'll stay up a while longer and then read something until I fall asleep."

He stares as I spread a sheet over the sofa. When I start to go for a pillow, he stands at the bedroom door, blocking the way.

"I'm going to ask you once more," he says. "What the hell do you think you're going to accomplish by this?"

"I need to be by myself tonight," I say. "I need to have time to think."

He lets out breath. "I'm thinking you're making a big mistake by doing this. I'm thinking you'd better think again about what you're doing. Claire?"

I can't answer. I don't know what I want to say. I turn and begin to tuck in the edges of the blanket. He stares at me a minute longer and then I see him raise his shoulders. "Suit yourself then. I could give a fuck less what you do," he says. He turns and walks down the hall scratching his neck.

This morning I read in the paper that services for Susan Miller are to be held in Chapel of the Pines, Summit, at two o'clock the next afternoon. Also, that police have taken statements from three people who saw her get into the green Chevrolet. But they still have no license number for the car. They are getting warmer, though, and the investigation is continuing. I sit for a long while holding the paper, thinking, then I call to make an appointment at the hairdresser's.

I sit under the dryer with a magazine on my lap and let Millie do my nails.

"I'm going to a funeral tomorrow," I say after we have talked a bit about a girl who no longer works there.

Millie looks up at me and then back at my fingers. "I'm sorry to hear that, Mrs. Kane. I'm real sorry."

"It's a young girl's funeral," I say.

"That's the worst kind. My sister died when I was a girl, and I'm still not over it to this day. Who died?" she says after a minute.

"A girl. We weren't all that close, you know, but still."

"Too bad. I'm real sorry. But we'll get you fixed up for it, don't worry. How's that look?"

"That looks . . . fine. Millie, did you ever wish you were somebody else, or else just nobody, nothing, nothing at all?"

She looks at me. "I can't say I ever felt that, no. No, if I was somebody else I'd be afraid I might not like who I was." She holds my fingers and seems to think about something for a minute. "I don't know, I just don't know. . . . Let me have your other hand now, Mrs. Kane."

At eleven o'clock that night I make another bed on the sofa and this time Stuart only looks at me, rolls his tongue behind his lips, and goes down the hall to the bedroom. In the night I wake and listen to the wind slamming the gate against the fence. I don't want to be awake, and I lie for a long while with my eyes closed. Finally I get up and go down the hall with my pillow. The light is burning in our bedroom and Stuart is on his back with his mouth open, breathing heavily. I go into Dean's room and get into bed with him. In his sleep he moves over to give me space. I lie there for a minute and then hold him, my face against his hair.

"What is it, Mama?" he says.

"Nothing, honey. Go back to sleep. It's nothing, it's all right."

I get up when I hear Stuart's alarm, put on coffee and prepare breakfast while he shaves.

He appears in the kitchen doorway, towel over his bare shoulder, appraising.

"Here's coffee," I say. "Eggs will be ready in a minute." He nods.

I wake Dean and the three of us have breakfast. Once or twice Stuart looks at me as if he wants to say something, but each time I ask Dean if he wants more milk, more toast, etc.

"I'll call you today," Stuart says as he opens the door.

"I don't think I'll be home today," I say quickly. "I have a lot of things to do today. In fact, I may be late for dinner."

"All right. Sure." He moves his briefcase from one hand to the other. "Maybe we'll go out for dinner tonight? How would you like that?" He keeps looking at me. He's forgotten about the girl already. "Are you all right?"

I move to straighten his tie, then drop my hand. He wants to kiss me goodbye. I move back a step. "Have a nice day then," he says finally. He turns and goes down the walk to his car.

I dress carefully. I try on a hat that I haven't worn in several years and look at myself in the mirror. Then I remove the hat, apply a light makeup, and write a note for Dean.

Honey, Mommy has things to do this afternoon, but will be home later. You are to stay in the house or in the back/yard until one of us comes home.
  Love

I look at the word "Love" and then I underline it. As I am writing the note I realize I don't know whether *back yard* is one word or two. I have never considered it before. I think about it and then I draw a line and make two words of it.

I stop for gas and ask directions to Summit. Barry, a forty-year-old mechanic with a moustache, comes out from the restroom and leans against the front fender while the other man, Lewis, puts the hose into the tank and begins to slowly wash the windshield.

"Summit," Barry says, looking at me and smoothing a finger down each side of his moustache. "There's no best way to get to Summit, Mrs. Kane. It's about a two-, two-and-a-half-hour drive each way. Across the mountains. It's quite a drive for a woman. Summit? What's in Summit, Mrs. Kane?"

"I have business," I say, vaguely uneasy. Lewis has gone to wait on another customer.

"Ah. Well, if I wasn't tied up there –" he gestures with his thumb toward the bay – "I'd offer to drive you to Summit and back again. Road's not all that good. I mean it's good enough, there's just a lot of curves and so on."

"I'll be all right. But thank you." He leans against the fender. I can feel his eyes as I open my purse.

Barry takes the credit card. "Don't drive it at night," he says. "It's not all that good a road, like I said. And while I'd be willing to bet you wouldn't have car trouble with this, I know this car, you can never be sure about blowouts and things like that. Just to be on the safe side I'd better check these tires." He taps one of the front tires with his shoe. "We'll run it onto the hoist. Won't take long."

"No, no, it's all right. Really, I can't take any more time. The tires look fine to me."

"Only takes a minute," he says. "Be on the safe side."

"I said no. No! They look fine to me. I have to go now. Barry. . . ."

"Mrs. Kane?"

"I have to go now."

I sign something. He gives me the receipt, the card, some

stamps. I put everything into my purse. "You take it easy," he says. "Be seeing you."

As I wait to pull into the traffic, I look back and see him watching. I close my eyes, then open them. He waves.

I turn at the first light, then turn again and drive until I come to the highway and read the sign: SUMMIT 117 MILES. It is ten-thirty and warm.

The highway skirts the edge of town, then passes through farm country, through fields of oats and sugar beets and apple orchards, with here and there a small herd of cattle grazing in open pastures. Then everything changes, the farms become fewer and fewer, more like shacks now than houses, and stands of timber replace the orchards. All at once I'm in the mountains and on the right, far below, I catch glimpses of the Naches River.

In a little while I see a green pickup truck behind me, and it stays behind me for miles. I keep slowing at the wrong times, hoping it will pass, and then increasing my speed, again at the wrong times. I grip the wheel until my fingers hurt. Then on a clear stretch he does pass, but he drives along beside for a minute, a crew-cut man in a blue workshirt in his early thirties, and we look at each other. Then he waves, toots the horn twice, and pulls ahead of me.

I slow down and find a place, a dirt road off of the shoulder. I pull over and turn off the ignition. I can hear the river somewhere down below the trees. Ahead of me the dirt road goes into the trees. Then I hear the pickup returning.

I start the engine just as the truck pulls up behind me. I lock the doors and roll up the windows. Perspiration breaks on my face and arms as I put the car in gear, but there is no place to drive.

"You all right?" the man says as he comes up to the car. "Hello. Hello in there." He raps the glass. "You okay?" He leans his arms on the door and brings his face close to the window.

I stare at him and can't find any words.

"After I passed I slowed up some," he says. "But when I didn't see you in the mirror I pulled off and waited a couple of minutes. When you still didn't show I thought I'd better drive back and check. Is everything all right? How come you're locked up in there?"

I shake my head.

"Come on, roll down your window. Hey, are you sure you're okay? You know it's not good for a woman to be batting around the country by herself." He shakes his head and looks at the highway, then back at me. "Now come on, roll down the window, how about it? We can't talk this way."

"Please, I have to go."

"Open the door, all right?" he says, as if he isn't listening. "At least roll the window down. You're going to smother in there." He looks at my breasts and legs. The skirt has pulled up over my knees. His eyes linger on my legs, but I sit still, afraid to move.

"I want to smother," I say. "I am smothering, can't you see?"

"What in the hell?" he says and moves back from the door. He turns and walks back to his truck. Then, in the side mirror, I watch him returning, and I close my eyes.

"You don't want me to follow you toward Summit or anything? I don't mind. I got some extra time this morning," he says.

I shake my head.

He hesitates and then shrugs. "Okay, lady, have it your way then," he says. "Okay."

I wait until he has reached the highway, and then I back

out. He shifts gears and pulls away slowly, looking back at me in his rearview mirror. I stop the car on the shoulder and put my head on the wheel.

The casket is closed and covered with floral sprays. The organ begins soon after I take a seat near the back of the chapel. People begin to file in and find chairs, some middle-aged and older people, but most of them in their early twenties or even younger. They are people who look uncomfortable in their suits and ties, sport coats and slacks, their dark dresses and leather gloves. One boy in flared pants and a yellow short-sleeved shirt takes the chair next to mine and begins to bite his lips. A door opens at one side of the chapel and I look up and for a minute the parking lot reminds me of a meadow. But then the sun flashes on car windows. The family enters in a group and moves into a curtained area off to the side. Chairs creak as they settle themselves. In a few minutes a slim, blond man in a dark suit stands and asks us to bow our heads. He speaks a brief prayer for us, the living, and when he finishes he asks us to pray in silence for the soul of Susan Miller, departed. I close my eyes and remember her picture in the newspaper and on television. I see her leaving the theater and getting into the green Chevrolet. Then I imagine her journey down the river, the nude body hitting rocks, caught at by branches, the body floating and turning, her hair streaming in the water. Then the hands and hair catching in the overhanging branches, holding, until four men come along to stare at her. I can see a man who is drunk (Stuart?) take her by the wrist. Does anyone here know about that? What if these people knew that? I look around at the other faces. There is a connection to be made of these things, these events, these faces, if I can find it. My head aches with the effort to find it.

89

He talks about Susan Miller's gifts: cheerfulness and beauty, grace and enthusiasm. From behind the closed curtain someone clears his throat, someone else sobs. The organ music begins. The service is over.

Along with the others I file slowly past the casket. Then I move out onto the front steps and into the bright, hot afternoon light. A middle-aged woman who limps as she goes down the stairs ahead of me reaches the sidewalk and looks around, her eyes falling on me. "Well, they got him," she says. "If that's any consolation. They arrested him this morning. I heard it on the radio before I came. A guy right here in town. A longhair, you might have guessed." We move a few steps down the hot sidewalk. People are starting cars. I put out my hand and hold on to a parking meter. Sunlight glances off polished hoods and fenders. My head swims. "He's admitted having relations with her that night, but he says he didn't kill her." She snorts. "They'll put him on probation and then turn him loose."

"He might not have acted alone," I say. "They'll have to be sure. He might be covering up for someone, a brother, or some friends."

"I have known that child since she was a little girl," the woman goes on, and her lips tremble. "She used to come over and I'd bake cookies for her and let her eat them in front of the TV." She looks off and begins shaking her head as the tears roll down her cheeks.

Stuart sits at the table with a drink in front of him. His eyes are red and for a minute I think he has been crying. He looks at me and doesn't say anything. For a wild instant I feel something has happened to Dean, and my heart turns.

"Where is he?" I say. "Where is Dean?"

"Outside," he says.

"Stuart, I'm so afraid, so afraid," I say, leaning against the door.

"What are you afraid of, Claire? Tell me, honey, and maybe I can help. I'd like to help, just try me. That's what husbands are for."

"I can't explain," I say. "I'm just afraid. I feel like, I feel like, I feel like. . . ."

He drains his glass and stands up, not taking his eyes from me. "I think I know what you need, honey. Let me play doctor, okay? Just take it easy now." He reaches an arm around my waist and with his other hand begins to unbutton my jacket, then my blouse. "First things first," he says, trying to joke.

"Not now, please," I say.

"Not now, please," he says, teasing. "Please nothing." Then he steps behind me and locks an arm around my waist. One of his hands slips under my brassiere.

"Stop, stop, stop," I say. I stamp on his toes.

And then I am lifted up and then falling. I sit on the floor looking up at him and my neck hurts and my skirt is over my knees. He leans down and says, "You go to hell then, do you hear, bitch? I hope your cunt drops off before I touch it again." He sobs once and I realize he can't help it, he can't help himself either. I feel a rush of pity for him as he heads for the living room.

He didn't sleep at home last night.

This morning, flowers, red and yellow chrysanthemums. I am drinking coffee when the doorbell rings.

"Mrs. Kane?" the young man says, holding his box of flowers.

I nod and pull the robe tighter at my throat.

"The man who called, he said you'd know." The boy looks at my robe, open at the throat, and touches his cap.

He stands with his legs apart, feet firmly planted on the top step. "Have a nice day," he says.

A little later the telephone rings and Stuart says, "Honey, how are you? I'll be home early, I love you. Did you hear me? I love you, I'm sorry, I'll make it up to you. Goodbye, I have to run now."

I put the flowers into a vase in the center of the dining room table and then I move my things into the extra bedroom.

Last night, around midnight, Stuart breaks the lock on my door. He does it just to show me that he can, I suppose, for he doesn't do anything when the door springs open except stand there in his underwear looking surprised and foolish while the anger slips from his face. He shuts the door slowly, and a few minutes later I hear him in the kitchen prying open a tray of ice cubes.

I'm in bed when he calls today to tell me that he's asked his mother to come stay with us for a few days. I wait a minute, thinking about this, and then hang up while he is still talking. But in a little while I dial his number at work. When he finally comes on the line I say, "It doesn't matter, Stuart. Really, I tell you it doesn't matter one way or the other."

"I love you," he says.

He says something else and I listen and nod slowly. I feel sleepy. Then I wake up and say, "For God's sake, Stuart, she was only a child."

A Small, Good Thing

SATURDAY AFTERNOON SHE DROVE to the bakery in the shopping center. After looking through a loose-leaf binder with photographs of cakes taped onto the pages, she ordered chocolate, the child's favorite. The cake she chose was decorated with a spaceship and launching pad under a sprinkling of white stars, and a planet made of red frosting at the other end. His name, SCOTTY, would be in green letters beneath the planet. The baker, who was an older man with a thick neck, listened without saying anything when she told him the child would be eight years old next Monday. The baker wore a white apron that looked like a smock. Straps cut under his arms, went around in back and then to the front again, where they were secured under his heavy waist. He wiped his hands on his apron as he listened to her. He kept his eyes down on the photographs and let her talk. He let her take her time. He'd just come to work and he'd be there all night, baking, and he was in no real hurry.

She gave the baker her name, Ann Weiss, and her telephone number. The cake would be ready on Monday morning, just out of the oven, in plenty of time for the child's party that afternoon. The baker was not jolly. There were no pleasantries between them, just the minimum exchange of words, the necessary information. He made her feel uncomfortable, and she didn't like that. While he was bent over the counter with the pencil in his hand, she studied his

coarse features and wondered if he'd ever done anything else
with his life besides be a baker. She was a mother and thirty-
three years old, and it seemed to her that everyone, especially
someone the baker's age – a man old enough to be her father
– must have children who'd gone through this special time
of cakes and birthday parties. There must be that between
them, she thought. But he was abrupt with her – not rude,
just abrupt. She gave up trying to make friends with him.
She looked into the back of the bakery and could see a long,
heavy wooden table with aluminum pie pans stacked at one
end; and beside the table a metal container filled with empty
racks. There was an enormous oven. A radio was playing
country-western music.

The baker finished printing the information on the special
order card and closed up the binder. He looked at her and
said, "Monday morning." She thanked him and drove home.

On Monday morning, the birthday boy was walking to
school with another boy. They were passing a bag of potato
chips back and forth and the birthday boy was trying to find
out what his friend intended to give him for his birthday that
afternoon. Without looking, the birthday boy stepped off the
curb at an intersection and was immediately knocked down
by a car. He fell on his side with his head in the gutter and
his legs out in the road. His eyes were closed, but his legs
moved back and forth as if he were trying to climb over
something. His friend dropped the potato chips and started
to cry. The car had gone a hundred feet or so and stopped
in the middle of the road. The man in the driver's seat looked
back over his shoulder. He waited until the boy got unstead-
ily to his feet. The boy wobbled a little. He looked dazed,
but okay. The driver put the car into gear and drove away.

The birthday boy didn't cry, but he didn't have anything

to say about anything either. He wouldn't answer when his friend asked him what it felt like to be hit by a car. He walked home, and his friend went on to school. But after the birthday boy was inside his house and was telling his mother about it – she sitting beside him on the sofa, holding his hands in her lap, saying, "Scotty, honey, are you sure you feel all right, baby?" thinking she would call the doctor anyway – he suddenly lay back on the sofa, closed his eyes, and went limp. When she couldn't wake him up, she hurried to the telephone and called her husband at work. Howard told her to remain calm, remain calm, and then he called an ambulance for the child and left for the hospital himself.

Of course, the birthday party was canceled. The child was in the hospital with a mild concussion and suffering from shock. There'd been vomiting, and his lungs had taken in fluid which needed pumping out that afternoon. Now he simply seemed to be in a very deep sleep – but no coma, Dr. Francis had emphasized, no coma, when he saw the alarm in the parents' eyes. At eleven o'clock that night, when the boy seemed to be resting comfortably enough after the many X-rays and the lab work, and it was just a matter of his waking up and coming around, Howard left the hospital. He and Ann had been at the hospital with the child since that afternoon, and he was going home for a short while to bathe and change clothes. "I'll be back in an hour," he said. She nodded. "It's fine," she said. "I'll be right here." He kissed her on the forehead, and they touched hands. She sat in the chair beside the bed and looked at the child. She was waiting for him to wake up and be all right. Then she could begin to relax.

Howard drove home from the hospital. He took the wet, dark streets very fast, then caught himself and slowed down. Until now, his life had gone smoothly and to his satisfaction – college, marriage, another year of college for the advanced degree in business, a junior partnership in an investment firm. Fatherhood. He was happy and, so far, lucky – he knew that. His parents were still living, his brothers and his sister were established, his friends from college had gone out to take their places in the world. So far, he had kept away from any real harm, from those forces he knew existed and that could cripple or bring down a man if the luck went bad, if things suddenly turned. He pulled into the driveway and parked. His left leg began to tremble. He sat in the car for a minute and tried to deal with the present situation in a rational manner. Scotty had been hit by a car and was in the hospital, but he was going to be all right. Howard closed his eyes and ran his hand over his face. He got out of the car and went up to the front door. The dog was barking inside the house. The telephone rang and rang while he unlocked the door and fumbled for the light switch. He shouldn't have left the hospital, he shouldn't have. "Goddamn it!" he said. He picked up the receiver and said, "I just walked in the door!"

"There's a cake here that wasn't picked up," the voice on the other end of the line said.

"What are you saying?" Howard asked.

"A cake," the voice said. "A sixteen-dollar cake."

Howard held the receiver against his ear, trying to understand. "I don't know anything about a cake," he said. "Jesus, what are you talking about?"

"Don't hand me that," the voice said.

Howard hung up the telephone. He went into the kitchen and poured himself some whiskey. He called the hospital. But the child's condition remained the same; he was still sleeping and nothing had changed there. While water poured into the tub, Howard lathered his face and shaved. He'd just stretched out in the tub and closed his eyes when the telephone rang again. He hauled himself out, grabbed a towel, and hurried through the house, saying, "Stupid, stupid," for having left the hospital. But when he picked up the receiver and shouted, "Hello!" there was no sound at the other end of the line. Then the caller hung up.

He arrived back at the hospital a little after midnight. Ann still sat in the chair beside the bed. She looked up at Howard, and then she looked back at the child. The child's eyes stayed closed, the head was still wrapped in bandages. His breathing was quiet and regular. From an apparatus over the bed hung a bottle of glucose with a tube running from the bottle to the boy's arm.

"How is he?" Howard said. "What's all this?" waving at the glucose and the tube.

"Dr. Francis's orders," she said. "He needs nourishment. He needs to keep up his strength. Why doesn't he wake up, Howard? I don't understand, if he's all right."

Howard put his hand against the back of her head. He ran his fingers through her hair. "He's going to be all right. He'll wake up in a little while. Dr. Francis knows what's what."

After a time, he said, "Maybe you should go home and get some rest. I'll stay here. Just don't put up with this creep who keeps calling. Hang up right away."

"Who's calling?" she asked.

"I don't know who, just somebody with nothing better to do than call up people. You go on now."

She shook her head. "No," she said, "I'm fine."

"Really," he said. "Go home for a while, and then come back and spell me in the morning. It'll be all right. What did Dr. Francis say? He said Scotty's going to be all right. We don't have to worry. He's just sleeping now, that's all."

A nurse pushed the door open. She nodded at them as she went to the bedside. She took the left arm out from under

the covers and put her fingers on the wrist, found the pulse,
then consulted her watch. In a little while, she put the arm
back under the covers and moved to the foot of the bed,
where she wrote something on a clipboard attached to the
bed.

"How is he?" Ann said. Howard's hand was a weight on
her shoulder. She was aware of the pressure from his fingers.

"He's stable," the nurse said. Then she said, "Doctor will
be in again shortly. Doctor's back in the hospital. He's
making rounds right now."

"I was saying maybe she'd want to go home and get a
little rest," Howard said. "After the doctor comes," he said.

"She could do that," the nurse said. "I think you should
both feel free to do that, if you wish." The nurse was a big
Scandinavian woman with blond hair. There was the trace
of an accent in her speech.

"We'll see what the doctor says," Ann said. "I want to
talk to the doctor. I don't think he should keep sleeping like
this. I don't think that's a good sign." She brought her hand
up to her eyes and let her head come forward a little.
Howard's grip tightened on her shoulder, and then his hand
moved up to her neck, where his fingers began to knead the
muscles there.

"Dr. Francis will be here in a few minutes," the nurse said.
Then she left the room.

Howard gazed at his son for a time, the small chest quietly
rising and falling under the covers. For the first time since
the terrible minutes after Ann's telephone call to him at his
office, he felt a genuine fear starting in his limbs. He began
shaking his head. Scotty was fine, but instead of sleeping at
home in his own bed, he was in a hospital bed with bandages
around his head and a tube in his arm. But this help was
what he needed right now.

Dr. Francis came in and shook hands with Howard,

though they'd just seen each other a few hours before. Ann got up from the chair. "Doctor?"

"Ann," he said and nodded. "Let's just first see how he's doing," the doctor said. He moved to the side of the bed and took the boy's pulse. He peeled back one eyelid and then the other. Howard and Ann stood beside the doctor and watched. Then the doctor turned back the covers and listened to the boy's heart and lungs with his stethoscope. He pressed his fingers here and there on the abdomen. When he was finished, he went to the end of the bed and studied the chart. He noted the time, scribbled something on the chart, and then looked at Howard and Ann.

"Doctor, how is he?" Howard said. "What's the matter with him exactly?"

"Why doesn't he wake up?" Ann said.

The doctor was a handsome, big-shouldered man with a tanned face. He wore a three-piece blue suit, a striped tie, and ivory cuff links. His gray hair was combed along the sides of his head, and he looked as if he had just come from a concert. "He's all right," the doctor said. "Nothing to shout about, he could be better, I think. But he's all right. Still, I wish he'd wake up. He should wake up pretty soon." The doctor looked at the boy again. "We'll know some more in a couple of hours, after the results of a few more tests are in. But he's all right, believe me, except for the hairline fracture of the skull. He does have that."

"Oh, no," Ann said.

"And a bit of a concussion, as I said before. Of course, you know he's in shock," the doctor said. "Sometimes you see this in shock cases. This sleeping."

"But he's out of any real danger?" Howard said. "You said before he's not in a coma. You wouldn't call this a coma, then – would you, doctor?" Howard waited. He looked at the doctor.

"No, I don't want to call it a coma," the doctor said and glanced over at the boy once more. "He's just in a very deep sleep. It's a restorative measure the body is taking on its own. He's out of any real danger, I'd say that for certain, yes. But we'll know more when he wakes up and the other tests are in," the doctor said.

"It's a coma," Ann said. "Of sorts."

"It's not a coma yet, not exactly," the doctor said. "I wouldn't want to call it coma. Not yet, anyway. He's suffered shock. In shock cases, this kind of reaction is common enough; it's a temporary reaction to bodily trauma. Coma. Well, coma is a deep, prolonged unconsciousness, something that could go on for days, or weeks even. Scotty's not in that area, not as far as we can tell. I'm certain his condition will show improvement by morning. I'm betting that it will. We'll know more when he wakes up, which shouldn't be long now. Of course, you may do as you like, stay here or go home for a time. But by all means feel free to leave the hospital for a while if you want. This is not easy, I know." The doctor gazed at the boy again, watching him, and then he turned to Ann and said, "You try not to worry, little mother. Believe me, we're doing all that can be done. It's just a question of a little more time now." He nodded at her, shook hands with Howard again, and then he left the room.

Ann put her hand over the child's forehead. "At least he doesn't have a fever," she said. Then she said, "My God, he feels so cold, though. Howard? Is he supposed to feel like this? Feel his head."

Howard touched the child's temples. His own breathing had slowed. "I think he's supposed to feel this way right now," he said. "He's in shock, remember? That's what the doctor said. The doctor was just in here. He would have said something if Scotty wasn't okay."

Ann stood there a while longer, working her lip with her

teeth. Then she moved over to her chair and sat down.

Howard sat in the chair next to her chair. They looked at each other. He wanted to say something else and reassure her, but he was afraid, too. He took her hand and put it in his lap, and this made him feel better, her hand being there. He picked up her hand and squeezed it. Then he just held her hand. They sat like that for a while, watching the boy and not talking. From time to time, he squeezed her hand. Finally, she took her hand away.

"I've been praying," she said.

He nodded.

She said, "I almost thought I'd forgotten how, but it came back to me. All I had to do was close my eyes and say, 'Please God, help us – help Scotty,' and then the rest was easy. The words were right there. Maybe if you prayed, too,". she said to him.

"I've already prayed," he said. "I prayed this afternoon – yesterday afternoon, I mean – after you called, while I was driving to the hospital. I've been praying," he said.

"That's good," she said. For the first time, she felt they were together in it, this trouble. She realized with a start that, until now, it had only been happening to her and to Scotty. She hadn't let Howard into it, though he was there and needed all along. She felt glad to be his wife.

The same nurse came in and took the boy's pulse again and checked the flow from the bottle hanging above the bed.

In an hour, another doctor came in. He said his name was Parsons, from Radiology. He had a bushy moustache. He was wearing loafers, a western shirt, and a pair of jeans.

"We're going to take him downstairs for more pictures," he told them. "We need to do some more pictures, and we want to do a scan."

"What's that?" Ann said. "A scan?" She stood between

this new doctor and the bed. "I thought you'd already taken all your X-rays."

"I'm afraid we need some more," he said. "Nothing to be alarmed about. We just need some more pictures, and we want to do a brain scan on him."

"My God," Ann said.

"It's perfectly normal procedure in cases like this," this new doctor said. "We just need to find out for sure why he isn't back awake yet. It's normal medical procedure, and nothing to be alarmed about. We'll be taking him down in a few minutes," this doctor said.

In a little while, two orderlies came into the room with a gurney. They were black-haired, dark-complexioned men in white uniforms, and they said a few words to each other in a foreign tongue as they unhooked the boy from the tube and moved him from his bed to the gurney. Then they wheeled him from the room. Howard and Ann got on the same elevator. Ann gazed at the child. She closed her eyes as the elevator began its descent. The orderlies stood at either end of the gurney without saying anything, though once one of the men made a comment to the other in their own language, and the other man nodded slowly in response.

Later that morning, just as the sun was beginning to lighten the windows in the waiting room outside the X-ray department, they brought the boy out and moved him back up to his room. Howard and Ann rode up on the elevator with him once more, and once more they took up their places beside the bed.

They waited all day, but still the boy did not wake up. Occasionally, one of them would leave the room to go down-stairs to the cafeteria to drink coffee and then, as if suddenly remembering and feeling guilty, get up from the table and

hurry back to the room. Dr. Francis came again that afternoon and examined the boy once more and then left after
telling them he was coming along and could wake up at any
minute now. Nurses, different nurses from the night before,
came in from time to time. Then a young woman from the
lab knocked and entered the room. She wore white slacks
and a white blouse and carried a little tray of things which
she put on the stand beside the bed. Without a word to them,
she took blood from the boy's arm. Howard closed his eyes
as the woman found the right place on the boy's arm and
pushed the needle in.

"I don't understand this," Ann said to the woman.

"Doctor's orders," the young woman said. "I do what I'm
told. They say draw that one, I draw. What's wrong with
him, anyway?" she said. "He's a sweetie."

"He was hit by a car," Howard said. "A hit-and-run."

The young woman shook her head and looked again at
the boy. Then she took her tray and left the room.

"Why won't he wake up?" Ann said. "Howard? I want
some answers from these people."

Howard didn't say anything. He sat down again in the
chair and crossed one leg over the other. He rubbed his face.
He looked at his son and then he settled back in the chair,
closed his eyes, and went to sleep.

Ann walked to the window and looked out at the parking
lot. It was night, and cars were driving into and out of the
parking lot with their lights on. She stood at the window
with her hands gripping the sill, and knew in her heart that
they were into something now, something hard. She was
afraid, and her teeth began to chatter until she tightened her
jaws. She saw a big car stop in front of the hospital and
someone, a woman in a long coat, get into the car. She
wished she were that woman and somebody, anybody, was
driving her away from here to somewhere else, a place where

she would find Scotty waiting for her when she stepped out of the car, ready to say *Mom* and let her gather him in her arms.

In a little while, Howard woke up. He looked at the boy again. Then he got up from the chair, stretched, and went over to stand beside her at the window. They both stared out at the parking lot. They didn't say anything. But they seemed to feel each other's insides now, as though the worry had made them transparent in a perfectly natural way.

The door opened and Dr. Francis came in. He was wearing a different suit and tie this time. His gray hair was combed along the sides of his head, and he looked as if he had just shaved. He went straight to the bed and examined the boy. "He ought to have come around by now. There's just no good reason for this," he said. "But I can tell you we're all convinced he's out of any danger. We'll just feel better when he wakes up. There's no reason, absolutely none, why he shouldn't come around. Very soon. Oh, he'll have himself a dilly of a headache when he does, you can count on that. But all of his signs are fine. They're as normal as can be."

"It is a coma, then?" Ann said.

The doctor rubbed his smooth cheek. "We'll call it that for the time being, until he wakes up. But you must be worn out. This is hard. I know this is hard. Feel free to go out for a bite," he said. "It would do you good. I'll put a nurse in here while you're gone if you'll feel better about going. Go and have yourselves something to eat."

"I couldn't eat anything," Ann said.

"Do what you need to do, of course," the doctor said. "Anyway, I wanted to tell you that all the signs are good, the tests are negative, nothing showed up at all, and just as soon as he wakes up he'll be over the hill."

"Thank you, doctor," Howard said. He shook hands with

the doctor again. The doctor patted Howard's shoulder and went out.

"I suppose one of us should go home and check on things," Howard said. "Slug needs to be fed, for one thing."

"Call one of the neighbors," Ann said. "Call the Morgans. Anyone will feed a dog if you ask them to."

"All right," Howard said. After a while, he said, "Honey, why don't *you* do it? Why don't you go home and check on things, and then come back? It'll do you good. I'll be right here with him. Seriously," he said. "We need to keep up our strength on this. We'll want to be here for a while even after he wakes up."

"Why don't *you* go?" she said. "Feed Slug. Feed yourself."

"I already went," he said. "I was gone for exactly an hour and fifteen minutes. You go home for an hour and freshen up. Then come back."

She tried to think about it, but she was too tired. She closed her eyes and tried to think about it again. After a time, she said, "Maybe I *will* go home for a few minutes. Maybe if I'm not just sitting right here watching him every second, he'll wake up and be all right. You know? Maybe he'll wake up if I'm not here. I'll go home and take a bath and put on clean clothes. I'll feed Slug. Then I'll come back."

"I'll be right here," he said. "You go on home, honey. I'll keep an eye on things here." His eyes were bloodshot and small, as if he'd been drinking for a long time. His clothes were rumpled. His beard had come out again. She touched his face, and then she took her hand back. She understood he wanted to be by himself for a while, not have to talk or share his worry for a time. She picked her purse up from the nightstand, and he helped her into her coat.

"I won't be gone long," she said.

"Just sit and rest for a little while when you get home," he said. "Eat something. Take a bath. After you get out of the bath, just sit for a while and rest. It'll do you a world of good, you'll see. Then come back," he said. "Let's try not to worry. You heard what Dr. Francis said."

She stood in her coat for a minute trying to recall the doctor's exact words, looking for any nuances, any hint of something behind his words other than what he had said. She tried to remember if his expression had changed any when he bent over to examine the child. She remembered the way his features had composed themselves as he rolled back the child's eyelids and then listened to his breathing.

She went to the door, where she turned and looked back. She looked at the child, and then she looked at the father. Howard nodded. She stepped out of the room and pulled the door closed behind her.

She went past the nurses' station and down to the end of the corridor, looking for the elevator. At the end of the corridor, she turned to her right and entered a little waiting room where a Negro family sat in wicker chairs. There was a middle-aged man in a khaki shirt and pants, a baseball cap pushed back on his head. A large woman wearing a house-dress and slippers was slumped in one of the chairs. A teen-aged girl in jeans, hair done in dozens of little braids, lay stretched out in one of the chairs smoking a cigarette, her legs crossed at the ankles. The family swung their eyes to Ann as she entered the room. The little table was littered with hamburger wrappers and Styrofoam cups.

"Franklin," the large woman said as she roused herself. "Is it about Franklin?" Her eyes widened. "Tell me now, lady," the woman said. "Is it about Franklin?" She was trying to rise from her chair, but the man had closed his hand over her arm.

"Here, here," he said. "Evelyn."

"I'm sorry," Ann said. "I'm looking for the elevator. My son is in the hospital, and now I can't find the elevator."

"Elevator is down that way, turn left," the man said as he aimed a finger.

The girl drew on her cigarette and stared at Ann. Her eyes were narrowed to slits, and her broad lips parted slowly as she let the smoke escape. The Negro woman let her head fall on her shoulder and looked away from Ann, no longer interested.

"My son was hit by a car," Ann said to the man. She seemed to need to explain herself. "He has a concussion and a little skull fracture, but he's going to be all right. He's in shock now, but it might be some kind of coma, too. That's what really worries us, the coma part. I'm going out for a little while, but my husband is with him. Maybe he'll wake up while I'm gone."

"That's too bad," the man said and shifted in the chair. He shook his head. He looked down at the table, and then he looked back at Ann. She was still standing there. He said, "Our Franklin, he's on the operating table. Somebody cut him. Tried to kill him. There was a fight where he was at. At this party. They say he was just standing and watching. Not bothering nobody. But that don't mean nothing these days. Now he's on the operating table. We're just hoping and praying, that's all we can do now." He gazed at her steadily.

Ann looked at the girl again, who was still watching her, and at the older woman, who kept her head down, but whose eyes were now closed. Ann saw the lips moving silently, making words. She had an urge to ask what those words were. She wanted to talk more with these people who were in the same kind of waiting she was in. She was afraid, and they were afraid. They had that in common. She would have liked to have said something else about the accident, told them more about Scotty, that it had happened on the day of his birthday, Monday, and that he was still unconscious. Yet she didn't know how to begin. She stood looking at them without saying anything more.

She went down the corridor the man had indicated and found the elevator. She waited a minute in front of the closed doors, still wondering if she was doing the right thing. Then she put out her finger and touched the button.

She pulled into the driveway and cut the engine. She closed her eyes and leaned her head against the wheel for a minute. She listened to the ticking sounds the engine made as it began to cool. Then she got out of the car. She could hear the dog barking inside the house. She went to the front door, which was unlocked. She went inside and turned on lights and put on a kettle of water for tea. She opened some dog food and fed Slug on the back porch. The dog ate in hungry little smacks. It kept running into the kitchen to see that she was going to stay. As she sat down on the sofa with her tea, the telephone rang.

"Yes!" she said as she answered. "Hello!"

"Mrs. Weiss," a man's voice said. It was five o'clock in the morning, and she thought she could hear machinery or equipment of some kind in the background.

"Yes, yes! What is it?" she said. "This is Mrs. Weiss. This is she. What is it, please?" She listened to whatever it was in the background. "Is it Scotty, for Christ's sake?"

"Scotty," the man's voice said. "It's about Scotty, yes. It has to do with Scotty, that problem. Have you forgotten about Scotty?" the man said. Then he hung up.

She dialed the hospital's number and asked for the third floor. She demanded information about her son from the nurse who answered the telephone. Then she asked to speak to her husband. It was, she said, an emergency.

She waited, turning the telephone cord in her fingers. She

closed her eyes and felt sick at her stomach. She would have to make herself eat. Slug came in from the back porch and lay down near her feet. He wagged his tail. She pulled at his ear while he licked her fingers. Howard was on the line.

"Somebody just called here," she said. She twisted the telephone cord. "He said it was about Scotty," she cried.

"Scotty's fine," Howard told her. "I mean, he's still sleeping. There's been no change. The nurse has been in twice since you've been gone. A nurse or else a doctor. He's all right."

"This man called. He said it was about Scotty," she told him.

"Honey, you rest for a little while, you need the rest. It must be that same caller I had. Just forget it. Come back down here after you've rested. Then we'll have breakfast or something."

"Breakfast," she said. "I don't want any breakfast."

"You know what I mean," he said. "Juice, something. I don't know. I don't know anything, Ann. Jesus, I'm not hungry, either. Ann, it's hard to talk now. I'm standing here at the desk. Dr. Francis is coming again at eight o'clock this morning. He's going to have something to tell us then, something more definite. That's what one of the nurses said. She didn't know any more than that. Ann? Honey, maybe we'll know something more then. At eight o'clock. Come back here before eight. Meanwhile, I'm right here and Scotty's all right. He's still the same," he added.

"I was drinking a cup of tea," she said, "when the telephone rang. They said it was about Scotty. There was a noise in the background. Was there a noise in the background on that call you had, Howard?"

"I don't remember," he said. "Maybe the driver of the car, maybe he's a psychopath and found out about Scotty somehow. But I'm here with him. Just rest like you were going to do. Take a bath and come back by seven or so, and we'll talk to the doctor together when he gets here. It's going to be all right, honey. I'm here, and there are doctors and nurses around. They say his condition is stable."

"I'm scared to death," she said.

She ran water, undressed, and got into the tub. She washed and dried quickly, not taking the time to wash her hair. She put on clean underwear, wool slacks, and a sweater. She went into the living room, where the dog looked up at her and let its tail thump once against the floor. It was just starting to get light outside when she went out to the car.

She drove into the parking lot of the hospital and found a space close to the front door. She felt she was in some obscure way responsible for what had happened to the child. She let her thoughts move to the Negro family. She remembered the name Franklin and the table that was covered with hamburger papers, and the teenaged girl staring at her as she drew on her cigarette. "Don't have children," she told the girl's image as she entered the front door of the hospital. "For God's sake, don't."

She took the elevator up to the third floor with two nurses who were just going on duty. It was Wednesday morning, a few minutes before seven. There was a page for a Dr. Madison as the elevator doors slid open on the third floor. She got off behind the nurses, who turned in the other direction and continued the conversation she had interrupted when she'd gotten into the elevator. She walked down the corridor to the little alcove where the Negro family had been waiting. They were gone now, but the chairs were scattered in such a way that it looked as if people had just jumped up from them the minute before. The tabletop was cluttered with the same cups and papers, the ashtray was filled with cigarette butts.

She stopped at the nurses' station. A nurse was standing behind the counter, brushing her hair and yawning.

"There was a Negro boy in surgery last night," Ann said. "Franklin was his name. His family was in the waiting room. I'd like to inquire about his condition."

A nurse who was sitting at a desk behind the counter looked up from a chart in front of her. The telephone buzzed and she picked up the receiver, but she kept her eyes on Ann.

"He passed away," said the nurse at the counter. The nurse held the hairbrush and kept looking at her. "Are you a friend of the family or what?"

"I met the family last night," Ann said. "My own son is in the hospital. I guess he's in shock. We don't know for sure what's wrong. I just wondered about Franklin, that's all. Thank you." She moved down the corridor. Elevator doors the same color as the walls slid open and a gaunt, bald man in white pants and white canvas shoes pulled a heavy cart off the elevator. She hadn't noticed these doors last night. The man wheeled the cart out into the corridor and stopped in front of the room nearest the elevator and consulted a clipboard. Then he reached down and slid a tray out of the cart. He rapped lightly on the door and entered the room. She could smell the unpleasant odors of warm food as she passed the cart. She hurried on without looking at any of the nurses and pushed open the door to the child's room.

Howard was standing at the window with his hands behind his back. He turned around as she came in.

"How is he?" she said. She went over to the bed. She dropped her purse on the floor beside the nightstand. It seemed to her she had been gone a long time. She touched the child's face. "Howard?"

"Dr. Francis was here a little while ago," Howard said. She looked at him closely and thought his shoulders were bunched a little.

"I thought he wasn't coming until eight o'clock this morning," she said quickly.

"There was another doctor with him. A neurologist."

"A neurologist," she said.

Howard nodded. His shoulders were bunching, she could see that. "What'd they say, Howard? For Christ's sake, what'd they say? What is it?"

"They said they're going to take him down and run more tests on him, Ann. They think they're going to operate, honey. Honey, they *are* going to operate. They can't figure out why he won't wake up. It's more than just shock or concussion, they know that much now. It's in his skull, the fracture, it has something, something to do with that, they think. So they're going to operate. I tried to call you, but I guess you'd already left the house."

"Oh, God," she said. "Oh, please, Howard, please," she said, taking his arms.

"Look!" Howard said. "Scotty! Look, Ann!" He turned her toward the bed.

The boy had opened his eyes, then closed them. He opened them again now. The eyes stared straight ahead for a minute, then moved slowly in his head until they rested on Howard and Ann, then traveled away again.

"Scotty," his mother said, moving to the bed.

"Hey, Scott," his father said. "Hey, son."

They leaned over the bed. Howard took the child's hand in his hands and began to pat and squeeze the hand. Ann bent over the boy and kissed his forehead again and again. She put her hands on either side of his face. "Scotty, honey, it's Mommy and Daddy," she said. "Scotty?"

The boy looked at them, but without any sign of recognition. Then his mouth opened, his eyes scrunched closed, and he howled until he had no more air in his lungs. His face seemed to relax and soften then. His lips parted as his last breath was puffed through his throat and exhaled gently through the clenched teeth.

The doctors called it a hidden occlusion and said it was a one-in-a-million circumstance. Maybe if it could have been detected somehow and surgery undertaken immediately, they could have saved him. But more than likely not. In any case, what would they have been looking for? Nothing had shown up in the tests or in the X-rays.

Dr. Francis was shaken. "I can't tell you how badly I feel. I'm so very sorry, I can't tell you," he said as he led them into the doctors' lounge. There was a doctor sitting in a chair with his legs hooked over the back of another chair, watching an early-morning TV show. He was wearing a green delivery-room outfit, loose green pants and green blouse, and a green cap that covered his hair. He looked at Howard and Ann and then looked at Dr. Francis. He got to his feet and turned off the set and went out of the room. Dr. Francis guided Ann to the sofa, sat down beside her, and began to talk in a low, consoling voice. At one point, he leaned over and embraced her. She could feel his chest rising and falling evenly against her shoulder. She kept her eyes open and let him hold her. Howard went into the bathroom, but he left the door open. After a violent fit of weeping, he ran water and washed his face. Then he came out and sat down at the little table that held a telephone. He looked at the telephone as though deciding what to do first. He made some calls. After a time, Dr. Francis used the telephone.

"Is there anything else I can do for the moment?" he asked them.

Howard shook his head. Ann stared at Dr. Francis as if unable to comprehend his words.

The doctor walked them to the hospital's front door. People were entering and leaving the hospital. It was eleven o'clock in the morning. Ann was aware of how slowly, almost reluctantly, she moved her feet. It seemed to her that Dr. Francis was making them leave when she felt they should stay, when it would be more the right thing to do to stay. She gazed out into the parking lot and then turned around and looked back at the front of the hospital. She began shaking her head. "No, no," she said. "I can't leave him here, no." She heard herself say that and thought how unfair it was that the only words that came out were the sort of words used on TV shows where people were stunned by violent or sudden deaths. She wanted her words to be her own. "No," she said, and for some reason the memory of the Negro woman's head lolling on the woman's shoulder came to her. "No," she said again.

"I'll be talking to you later in the day," the doctor was saying to Howard. "There are still some things that have to be done, things that have to be cleared up to our satisfaction. Some things that need explaining."

"An autopsy," Howard said.

Dr. Francis nodded.

"I understand," Howard said. Then he said, "Oh, Jesus. No, I don't understand, doctor. I can't, I can't. I just can't."

Dr. Francis put his arm around Howard's shoulders. "I'm sorry. God, how I'm sorry." He let go of Howard's shoulders and held out his hand. Howard looked at the hand, and then he took it. Dr. Francis put his arms around Ann once more. He seemed full of some goodness she didn't understand. She let her head rest on his shoulder, but her eyes stayed open. She kept looking at the hospital. As they drove out of the parking lot, she looked back at the hospital.

★   ★   ★

At home, she sat on the sofa with her hands in her coat pockets. Howard closed the door to the child's room. He got the coffee-maker going and then he found an empty box. He had thought to pick up some of the child's things that were scattered around the living room. But instead he sat down beside her on the sofa, pushed the box to one side, and leaned forward, arms between his knees. He began to weep. She pulled his head over into her lap and patted his shoulder. "He's gone," she said. She kept patting his shoulder. Over his sobs, she could hear the coffee-maker hissing in the kitchen. "There, there," she said tenderly. "Howard, he's gone. He's gone and now we'll have to get used to that. To being alone."

In a little while, Howard got up and began moving aimlessly around the room with the box, not putting anything into it, but collecting some things together on the floor at one end of the sofa. She continued to sit with her hands in her coat pockets. Howard put the box down and brought coffee into the living room. Later, Ann made calls to relatives. After each call had been placed and the party had answered, Ann would blurt out a few words and cry for a minute. Then she would quietly explain, in a measured voice, what had happened and tell them about arrangements. Howard took the box out to the garage, where he saw the child's bicycle. He dropped the box and sat down on the pavement beside the bicycle. He took hold of the bicycle awkwardly so that it leaned against his chest. He held it, the rubber pedal sticking into his chest. He gave the wheel a turn.

Ann hung up the telephone after talking to her sister. She was looking up another number when the telephone rang. She picked it up on the first ring.

"Hello," she said, and she heard something in the background, a humming noise. "Hello!" she said. "For God's sake," she said. "Who is this? What is it you want?"

"Your Scotty, I got him ready for you," the man's voice said. "Did you forget him?"

"You evil bastard!" she shouted into the receiver. "How can you do this, you evil son of a bitch?"

"Scotty," the man said. "Have you forgotten about Scotty?" Then the man hung up on her.

Howard heard the shouting and came in to find her with her head on her arms over the table, weeping. He picked up the receiver and listened to the dial tone.

Much later, just before midnight, after they had dealt with many things, the telephone rang again.

"You answer it," she said. "Howard, it's him, I know." They were sitting at the kitchen table with coffee in front of them. Howard had a small glass of whiskey beside his cup. He answered on the third ring.

"Hello," he said. "Who is this? Hello! Hello!" The line went dead. "He hung up," Howard said. "Whoever it was."

"It was him," she said. "That bastard. I'd like to kill him," she said. "I'd like to shoot him and watch him kick," she said.

"Ann, my God," he said.

"Could you hear anything?" she said. "In the background? A noise, machinery, something humming?"

"Nothing, really. Nothing like that," he said. "There wasn't much time. I think there was some radio music. Yes, there was a radio going, that's all I could tell. I don't know what in God's name is going on," he said.

She shook her head. "If I could, could get my hands on him." It came to her then. She knew who it was. Scotty, the cake, the telephone number. She pushed the chair away from the table and got up. "Drive me down to the shopping center," she said. "Howard."

"What are you saying?"

"The shopping center. I know who it is who's calling. I know who it is. It's the baker, the son-of-a-bitching baker, Howard. I had him bake a cake for Scotty's birthday. That's who's calling. That's who has the number and keeps calling us. To harass us about that cake. The baker, that bastard."

They drove down to the shopping center. The sky was clear and stars were out. It was cold, and they ran the heater in the car. They parked in front of the bakery. All of the shops and stores were closed, but there were cars at the far end of the lot in front of the movie theater. The bakery windows were dark, but when they looked through the glass they could see a light in the back room and, now and then, a big man in an apron moving in and out of the white, even light. Through the glass, she could see the display cases and some little tables with chairs. She tried the door. She rapped on the glass. But if the baker heard them, he gave no sign. He didn't look in their direction.

They drove around behind the bakery and parked. They got out of the car. There was a lighted window too high up for them to see inside. A sign near the back door said THE PANTRY BAKERY, SPECIAL ORDERS. She could hear faintly a radio playing inside and something creak – an oven door as it was pulled down? She knocked on the door and waited. Then she knocked again, louder. The radio was turned down and there was a scraping sound now, the distinct sound of something, a drawer, being pulled open and then closed.

Someone unlocked the door and opened it. The baker stood in the light and peered out at them. "I'm closed for business," he said. "What do you want at this hour? It's midnight. Are you drunk or something?"

She stepped into the light that fell through the open door. He blinked his heavy eyelids as he recognized her. "It's you," he said.

"It's me," she said. "Scotty's mother. This is Scotty's father. We'd like to come in."

The baker said, "I'm busy now. I have work to do."

She had stepped inside the doorway anyway. Howard came in behind her. The baker moved back. "It smells like a bakery in here. Doesn't it smell like a bakery in here, Howard?"

"What do you want?" the baker said. "Maybe you want your cake? That's it, you decided you want your cake. You ordered a cake, didn't you?"

"You're pretty smart for a baker," she said. "Howard, this is the man who's been calling us." She clenched her fists. She stared at him fiercely. There was a deep burning inside her, an anger that made her feel larger than herself, larger than either of these men.

"Just a minute here," the baker said. "You want to pick up your three-day-old cake? That it? I don't want to argue with you, lady. There it sits over there, getting stale. I'll give it to you for half of what I quoted you. No. You want it? You can have it. It's no good to me, no good to anyone now. It cost me time and money to make that cake. If you want it, okay, if you don't, that's okay, too. I have to get back to work." He looked at them and rolled his tongue behind his teeth.

"More cakes," she said. She knew she was in control of it, of what was increasing in her. She was calm.

"Lady, I work sixteen hours a day in this place to earn a living," the baker said. He wiped his hands on his apron. "I work night and day in here, trying to make ends meet." A look crossed Ann's face that made the baker move back and say, "No trouble, now." He reached to the counter and picked up a rolling pin with his right hand and began to tap it against the palm of his other hand. "You want the cake or not? I have to get back to work. Bakers work at night," he said again. His eyes were small, mean-looking, she thought, nearly lost in the bristly flesh around his cheeks. His neck was thick with fat.

"I know bakers work at night," Ann said. "They make phone calls at night, too. You bastard," she said.

The baker continued to tap the rolling pin against his hand. He glanced at Howard. "Careful, careful," he said to Howard.

"My son's dead," she said with a cold, even finality. "He was hit by a car Monday morning. We've been waiting with him until he died. But, of course, you couldn't be expected to know that, could you? Bakers can't know everything – can they, Mr. Baker? But he's dead. He's dead, you bastard!" Just as suddenly as it had welled in her, the anger dwindled, gave way to something else, a dizzy feeling of nausea. She leaned against the wooden table that was sprinkled with flour, put her hands over her face, and began to cry, her shoulders rocking back and forth. "It isn't fair," she said. "It isn't, isn't fair."

Howard put his hand at the small of her back and looked at the baker. "Shame on you," Howard said to him. "Shame."

The baker put the rolling pin back on the counter. He undid his apron and threw it on the counter. He looked at them, and then he shook his head slowly. He pulled a chair out from under the card table that held papers and receipts, an adding machine, and a telephone directory. "Please sit down," he said. "Let me get you a chair," he said to Howard. "Sit down now, please." The baker went into the front of the shop and returned with two little wrought-iron chairs. "Please sit down, you people."

Ann wiped her eyes and looked at the baker. "I wanted to kill you," she said. "I wanted you dead."

The baker had cleared a space for them at the table. He shoved the adding machine to one side, along with the stacks of notepaper and receipts. He pushed the telephone directory onto the floor, where it landed with a thud. Howard and Ann sat down and pulled their chairs up to the table. The baker sat down, too.

"Let me say how sorry I am," the baker said, putting his elbows on the table. "God alone knows how sorry. Listen to me. I'm just a baker. I don't claim to be anything else. Maybe once, maybe years ago, I was a different kind of human being. I've forgotten, I don't know for sure. But I'm not any longer, if I ever was. Now I'm just a baker. That don't excuse my doing what I did, I know. But I'm deeply sorry. I'm sorry for your son, and sorry for my part in this," the baker said. He spread his hands out on the table and turned them over to reveal his palms. "I don't have any children myself, so I can only imagine what you must be feeling. All I can say to you now is that I'm sorry. Forgive me, if you can," the baker said. "I'm not an evil man, I don't think. Not evil, like you said on the phone. You got to understand what it comes down to is I don't know how to act anymore, it would seem. Please," the man said, "let me ask you if you can find it in your hearts to forgive me?"

It was warm inside the bakery. Howard stood up from the table and took off his coat. He helped Ann from her coat. The baker looked at them for a minute and then nodded and got up from the table. He went to the oven and turned off some switches. He found cups and poured coffee from an electric coffee-maker. He put a carton of cream on the table, and a bowl of sugar.

"You probably need to eat something," the baker said. "I hope you'll eat some of my hot rolls. You have to eat and keep going. Eating is a small, good thing in a time like this," he said.

He served them warm cinnamon rolls just out of the oven, the icing still runny. He put butter on the table and knives to spread the butter. Then the baker sat down at the table with them. He waited. He waited until they each took a roll from the platter and began to eat. "It's good to eat something," he said, watching them. "There's more. Eat up. Eat all you want. There's all the rolls in the world in here."

They ate rolls and drank coffee. Ann was suddenly hungry, and the rolls were warm and sweet. She ate three of them, which pleased the baker. Then he began to talk. They listened carefully. Although they were tired and in anguish, they listened to what the baker had to say. They nodded when the baker began to speak of loneliness, and of the sense of doubt and limitation that had come to him in his middle years. He told them what it was like to be childless all these years. To repeat the days with the ovens endlessly full and endlessly empty. The party food, the celebrations he'd worked over. Icing knuckle-deep. The tiny wedding couples stuck into cakes. Hundreds of them, no, thousands by now. Birthdays. Just imagine all those candles burning. He had a necessary trade. He was a baker. He was glad he wasn't a florist. It was better to be feeding people. This was a better smell anytime than flowers.

"Smell this," the baker said, breaking open a dark loaf. "It's a heavy bread, but rich." They smelled it, then he had them taste it. It had the taste of molasses and coarse grains. They listened to him. They ate what they could. They swallowed the dark bread. It was like daylight under the fluorescent trays of light. They talked on into the early morning, the high, pale cast of light in the windows, and they did not think of leaving.

Jerry and Molly and Sam

AS AL SAW IT, there was only one solution. He had to get rid of the dog without Betty or the kids finding out about it. At night. It would have to be done at night. He would simply drive Suzy – well, someplace, later he'd decide where – open the door, push her out, drive away. The sooner the better. He felt relieved making the decision. Any action was better than no action at all, he was becoming convinced.

It was Sunday. He got up from the kitchen table where he had been eating a late breakfast by himself and stood by the sink, hands in his pockets. Nothing was going right lately. He had enough to contend with without having to worry about a stinking dog. They were laying off at Aerojet when they should be hiring. The middle of the summer, defense contracts let all over the country and Aerojet was talking of cutting back. *Was* cutting back, in fact, a little more every day. He was no safer than anyone else even though he'd been there two years going on three. He got along with the right people, all right, but seniority or friendship, either one, didn't mean a damn these days. If your number was up, that was that – and there was nothing anybody could do. They got ready to lay off, they laid off. Fifty, a hundred men at a time.

No one was safe, from the foreman and supers right on down to the man on the line. And three months ago, just before all the layoffs began, he'd let Betty talk him moving into this cushy two-hundred-a-month place. Lease, with an option to buy. Shit!

Al hadn't really wanted to leave the other place. He had been comfortable enough. Who could know that two weeks after he'd move they'd start laying off? But who could know anything these days? For example, there was Jill. Jill worked in bookkeeping at Weinstock's. She was a nice girl, said she loved Al. She was just lonely, that's what she told him the first night. She didn't make it a habit, letting herself be picked up by married men, she also told him the first night. He'd met Jill about three months ago, when he was feeling depressed and jittery with all the talk of layoffs just beginning. He met her at the Town and Country, a bar not too far from his new place. They danced a little and he drove her home and they necked in the car in front of her apartment. He had not gone upstairs with her that night, though he was sure he could have. He went upstairs with her the next night.

Now he was having an *affair*, for Christ's sake, and he didn't know what to do about it. He did not want it to go on, and he did not want to break it off: you don't throw everything overboard in a storm. Al was drifting, and he knew he was drifting, and where it was all going to end he could not guess at. But he was beginning to feel he was losing control over everything. Everything. Recently, too, he had caught himself thinking about old age after he'd been constipated a few days – an affliction he had always associated with the elderly. Then there was the matter of the tiny bald spot and of his having just begun to wonder how he would comb his hair a different way. What was he going to do with his life? he wanted to know.

He was thirty-one.

All these things to contend with and then *Sandy*, his wife's younger sister, giving the kids, Alex and Mary, that mongrel dog about four months ago. He wished he'd never seen that dog. Or Sandy, either, for that matter. That bitch! She was always turning up with some shit or other that wound up costing him money, some little flimflam that went haywire after a day or two and *had* to be repaired, something the kids could scream over and fight over and beat the shit out of each other about. God! And then turning right around to touch him, through *Betty*, for twenty-five bucks. The mere thought of all the twenty-five- or fifty-buck checks, and the one just a few months ago for eighty-five to make her car payment – her *car* payment, for God's sake, when he didn't even know if he was going to have a roof over his head – made him want to *kill* the goddamn dog.

Sandy! Betty and Alex and Mary! Jill! And Suzy the goddamn dog!

This was Al.

He had to start someplace – setting things in order, sorting all this out. It was time to do something, time for some straight thinking for a change. And he intended to start tonight.

He would coax the dog into the car undetected and, on some pretext or another, go out. Yet he hated to think of the way Betty would lower her eyes as she watched him dress, and then, later, just before he went out the door, ask him where, how long, etc., in a resigned voice that made him feel all the worse. He could never get used to the lying. Besides, he hated to use what little reserve he might have left with Betty by telling her a lie for something different from what she suspected. A wasted lie, so to speak. But he could not tell her the truth, could not say he was *not* going drinking, was *not* going calling on somebody, was instead going to do away with the goddamn dog and thus take the first step toward setting his house in order.

He ran his hand over his face, tried to put it all out of his mind for a minute. He took out a cold half quart of Lucky from the fridge and popped the aluminum top. His life had become a maze, one lie overlaid upon another until he was not sure he could untangle them if he had to.

"The goddamn dog," he said out loud.

"She doesn't have good sense!" was how Al put it. She was a sneak, besides. The moment the back door was left open and everyone gone, she'd pry open the screen, come through to the living room, and urinate on the carpet. There were at least a half dozen map-shaped stains on it right now. But her favorite place was the utility room, where she could root in the dirty clothes, so that all of the shorts and panties now had crotch or seat chewed away. And she chewed through the antenna wires on the outside of the house, and once Al pulled into the drive and found her lying in the front yard with one of his Florsheims in her mouth.

"She's crazy," he'd say. "And she's driving me crazy. I can't make it fast enough to replace it. The sonofabitch, I'm going to kill her one of these days!"

Betty tolerated the dog at greater durations, would go along apparently unruffled for a time, but suddenly she would come upon it, with fists clenched, call it a bastard, a bitch, shriek at the kids about keeping it out of their room, the living room, etc. Betty was that way with the children, too. She could go along with them just so far, let them get away with just so much, and then she would turn on them savagely and slap their faces, screaming, "Stop it! Stop it! I can't stand any more of it!"

But then Betty would say, "It's their first dog. You remember how fond you must have been of your first dog."

"My dog had brains," he would say. "It was an Irish setter!"

*   *   *

The afternoon passed. Betty and the kids returned from someplace or another in the car, and they all had sandwiches and potato chips on the patio. He fell asleep on the grass, and when he woke it was nearly evening.

He showered, shaved, put on slacks and a clean shirt. He felt rested but sluggish. He dressed and he thought of Jill. He thought of Betty and Alex and Mary and Sandy and Suzy. He felt drugged.

"We'll have supper pretty soon," Betty said, coming to the bathroom door and staring at him.

"That's all right. I'm not hungry. Too hot to eat," he said fiddling with his shirt collar. "I might drive over to Carl's, shoot a few games of pool, have a couple of beers."

She said, "I see."

He said, "Jesus!"

She said, "Go ahead, I don't care."

He said, "I won't be gone long."

She said, "Go ahead, I said. I said I don't care."

In the garage, he said, "Goddamn you all!" and kicked the rake across the cement floor. Then he lit a cigarette and tried to get hold of himself. He picked up the rake and put it away where it belonged. He was muttering to himself, saying, "Order, order," when the dog came up to the garage, sniffed around the door, and looked in.

"Here. Come here, Suzy. Here, girl," he called.

The dog wagged her tail but stayed where she was.

He went over to the cupboard above the lawn mower and took down one, then two, and finally three cans of food.

"All you want tonight, Suzy, old girl. All you can eat," he coaxed, opening up both ends of the first can and sliding the mess into the dog's dish.

★   ★   ★

He drove around for nearly an hour, not able to decide on a place. If he dropped her off in just any neighborhood and the pound were called, the dog would be back in the house in a day or two. The county pound was the first place Betty would call. He remembered reading stories about lost dogs finding their way hundreds of miles back home again. He remembered crime programs where someone saw a license number, and the thought made his heart jump. Held up to public view, without all the facts being in, it'd be a shameful thing to be caught abandoning a dog. He would have to find the right place.

He drove over near the American River. The dog needed to get out more anyway, get the feel of the wind on its back, be able to swim and wade in the river when it wanted; it was a pity to keep a dog fenced in all the time. But the fields near the levee seemed too desolate, no houses around at all. After all, he did want the dog to be found and cared for. A large old two-story house was what he had in mind, with happy, well-behaved reasonable children who needed a dog, who desperately needed a dog. But there were no old two-story houses here, not a one.

He drove back onto the highway. He had not been able to look at the dog since he'd managed to get her into the car. She lay quietly on the back seat now. But when he pulled off the road and stopped the car, she sat up and whined, looking around.

He stopped at a bar, rolled all the car windows down before he went inside. He stayed nearly an hour, drinking beer and playing the shuffleboard. He kept wondering if he should have left all the doors ajar too. When he went back outside, Suzy sat up in the seat and rolled her lips back, showing her teeth.

He got in and started off again.

★ ★ ★

Then he thought of the place. The neighborhood where they used to live, swarming with kids and just across the line in Yolo County, that would be just the right place. If the dog were picked up, it would be taken to the Woodland Pound, not the pound in Sacramento. Just drive onto one of the streets in the old neighborhood, stop, throw out a handful of the shit she ate, open the door, a little assistance in the way of a push, and out she'd go while he took off. Done! It would be done.

He stepped on it getting out there.

There were porch lights on and at three or four houses he saw men and women sitting on the front steps as he drove by. He cruised along, and when he came to his old house he slowed down almost to a stop and stared at the front door, the porch, the lighted windows. He felt even more insubstantial, looking at the house. He had lived there – how long? A year, sixteen months? Before that, Chico, Red Bluff, Tacoma, Portland – where he'd met Betty – Yakima . . . Toppenish, where he was born and went to high school. Not since he was a kid, it seemed to him, had he known what it was to be free from worry and worse. He thought of summers fishing and camping in the Cascades, autumns when he'd hunt pheasants behind Sam, the setter's flashing red coat a beacon through cornfields and alfalfa meadows where the boy that he was and the dog that he had would both run like mad. He wished he could keep driving and driving tonight until he was driving onto the old bricked main street of Toppenish, turning left at the first light, then left again, stopping when he came to where his mother lived, and never, never, for any reason ever, ever leave again.

He came to the darkened end of the street. There was a large empty field straight ahead and the street turned to the right, skirting it. For almost a block there were no houses on the side nearer the field and only one house, completely dark, on the other side. He stopped the car and, without thinking any longer about what he was doing, scooped a handful of dog food up, leaned over the seat, opened the back door nearer the field, threw the stuff out, and said, "Go on, Suzy." He pushed her until she jumped down reluctantly. He leaned over farther, pulled the door shut, and drove off, slowly. Then he drove faster and faster.

He stopped at Dupee's, the first bar he came to on the way back to Sacramento. He was jumpy and perspiring. He didn't feel exactly unburdened or relieved, as he had thought he would feel. But he kept assuring himself it was a step in the right direction, that the good feeling would settle on him tomorrow. The thing to do was to wait it out.

After four beers a girl in a turtleneck sweater and sandals and carrying a suitcase sat down beside him. She set the suitcase between the stools. She seemed to know the bartender, and the bartender had something to say to her whenever he came by, once or twice stopping briefly to talk. She told Al her name was Molly, but she wouldn't let him buy her a beer. Instead, she offered to eat half a pizza.

He smiled at her, and she smiled back. He took out his cigarettes and his lighter and put them on the bar.

"Pizza it is!" he said.

Later, he said, "Can I give you a lift somewhere?"

"No, thanks. I'm waiting for someone," she said.

He said, "Where you heading for?"

She said, "No place. Oh," she said, touching the suitcase with her toe, "you mean that?" laughing. "I live here in West Sac. I'm not going anyplace. It's just a washing-machine motor inside belongs to my mother. Jerry – that's the bartender – he's good at fixing things. Jerry said he'd fix it for nothing."

Al got up. He weaved a little as he leaned over her. He said, "Well, goodbye, honey. I'll see you around."

"You bet!" she said. "And thanks for the pizza. Hadn't eaten since lunch. Been trying to take some of this off." She raised her sweater, gathered a handful of flesh at the waist.

"Sure I can't give you a lift someplace?" he said.

The woman shook her head.

In the car again, driving, he reached for his cigarettes and then, frantically, for his lighter, remembering leaving everything on the bar. The hell with it, he thought, let her have it. Let her put the lighter and the cigarettes in the suitcase along with the washing machine. He chalked it up against the dog, one more expense. But the last, by God! It angered him now, now that he was getting things in order, that the girl hadn't been more friendly. If he'd been in a different frame of mind, he could have picked her up. But when you're depressed, it shows all over you, even the way you light a cigarette.

He decided to go see Jill. He stopped at a liquor store and bought a pint of whiskey and climbed the stairs to her apartment and he stopped at the landing to catch his breath and to clean his teeth with his tongue. He could still taste the mushrooms from the pizza, and his mouth and throat were seared from the whiskey. He realized that what he wanted to do was to go right to Jill's bathroom and use her toothbrush.

He knocked. "It's me, Al," he whispered. "Al," he said louder. He heard her feet hit the floor. She threw the lock and then tried to undo the chain as he leaned heavily against the door.

"Just a minute, honey. Al, you'll have to quit pushing – I can't unhook it. There," she said and opened the door, scanning his face as she took him by the hand.

The embraced clumsily, and he kissed her on the cheek.

"Sit down, honey. Here." She switched on a lamp and helped him to the couch. Then she touched her fingers to her curlers and said, "I'll put on some lipstick. What would you like in the meantime? Coffee? Juice? A beer? I think I have some beer. What do you have there . . . whiskey? What would you like, honey?" She stroked his hair with one hand and leaned over him, gazing into his eyes. "Poor baby, what would you like?" she said.

"Just want you hold me," he said. "Here. Sit down. No lipstick," he said, pulling her onto his lap. "Hold. I'm falling," he said.

She put an arm around his shoulders. She said, "You come on over to the bed, baby, I'll give you what you like."

"Tell you, Jill," he said, "skating on thin ice. Crash through any minute . . . I don't know." He stared at her with a fixed, puffy expression that he could feel but not correct. "Serious," he said.

She nodded. "Don't think about anything, baby. Just relax," she said. She pulled his face to hers and kissed him on the forehead and then the lips. She turned slightly on his lap and said, "No, don't move, Al," the fingers of both hands suddenly slipping around the back of his neck and gripping his face at the same time. His eyes wobbled around the room an instant, then tried to focus on what she was doing. She held his head in place in her strong fingers. With her thumbnails she was squeezing out a blackhead to the side of his nose.

"Sit still!" she said.

"No," he said. "Don't! Stop! Not in the mood for that."

"I almost have it. Sit still, I said! . . . There, look at that. What do you think of that? Didn't know that was there, did

you? Now just one more, a big one, baby. The last one,"
she said.

"Bathroom," he said, forcing her off, freeing his way.

At home it was all tears, confusion. Mary ran out to the car,
crying, before he could get parked.

"Suzy's gone," she sobbed. "Suzy's gone. She's never
coming back, Daddy, I know it. She's gone!"

My God, heart lurching. *What have I done?*

"Now don't worry, sweetheart. She's probably just off
running around somewhere. She'll be back," he said.

"She isn't, Daddy. I know she isn't. Mama said we may
have to get another dog."

"Wouldn't that be all right, honey?" he said. "Another
dog, if Suzy doesn't come back? We'll go to the pet store – "

"I don't want another dog!" the child cried, holding onto
his leg.

"Can we have a monkey, Daddy, instead of a dog?" Alex
asked. "If we go to the pet store to look for a dog, can we
have a monkey instead?"

"I don't want a monkey!" Mary cried. "I want Suzy."

"Everybody let go now, let Daddy in the house. Daddy
has a terrible, terrible headache," he said.

Betty lifted a casserole dish from the oven. She looked
tired, irritable . . . older. She didn't look at him. "The kids
tell you? Suzy's gone? I've combed the neighborhood. Every-
where, I swear."

"That dog'll turn up," he said. "Probably just running
around somewhere. That dog'll come back," he said.

"Seriously," she said, turning to him with her hands on
her hips, "I think it's something else. I think she might have
got hit by a car. I want you to drive around. The kids called
her last night, and she was gone then. That's the last's been

seen of her. I called the pound and described her to them, but they said all their trucks aren't in yet. I'm supposed to call again in the morning."

He went into the bathroom and could hear her still going on. He began to run the water in the sink, wondering, with a fluttery sensation in his stomach, how grave exactly was his mistake. When he turned off the faucets, he could still hear her. He kept staring at the sink.

"Did you hear me?" she called. "I want you to drive around and look for her after supper. The kids can go with you and look too . . . Al?"

"Yes, yes," he answered.

"What?" she said. "What'd you say?"

"I said yes. Yes! All right. Anything! Just let me wash up first, will you?"

She looked through from the kitchen. "Well, what in the hell is eating you? I didn't ask you to get drunk last night, did I? I've had enough of it, I can tell you! I've had a hell of a day, if you want to know. Alex waking me up at five this morning getting in with me, telling me his daddy was snoring so loud that . . . that you *scared* him! I saw you out there with your clothes on passed out and the room smelling to high heaven. I tell you, I've had enough of it!" She looked around the kitchen quickly, as if to seize something.

He kicked the door shut. Everything was going to hell. While he was shaving, he stopped once and held the razor in his hand and looked at himself in the mirror: his face doughy, characterless – *immoral*, that was the word. He laid the razor down. *I believe I have made the gravest mistake this time. I believe I have made the gravest mistake of all.* He brought the razor up to his throat and finished.

★ ★ ★

He did not shower, did not change clothes. "Put my supper in the oven for me," he said. "Or in the refrigerator. I'm going out. Right now," he said.

"You can wait till after supper. The kids can go with you."

"No, the hell with that. Let the kids eat supper, look around here if they want. I'm not hungry, and it'll be dark soon."

"Is everybody going crazy?" she said. "I don't know what's going to happen to us. I'm ready for a nervous breakdown. I'm ready to lose my mind. What's going to happen to the kids if I lose my mind?" She slumped against the draining board, her face crumpled, tears rolling off her cheeks. "You don't love them, anyway! You never have. It isn't the dog I'm worried about. It's us! It's us! I know you don't love me any more – goddamn you! – but you don't even love the kids!"

"Betty, Betty!" he said. "My God!" he said. "Everything's going to be all right. I promise you," he said. "Don't worry," he said. "I promise you, things'll be all right. I'll find the dog and then things will be all right," he said.

He bounded out of the house, ducked into the bushes as he heard his children coming: the girl crying, saying, "Suzy, Suzy"; the boy saying maybe a train ran over her. When they were inside the house, he made a break for the car.

He fretted at all the lights he had to wait for, bitterly resented the time lost when he stopped for gas. The sun was low and heavy, just over the squat range of hills at the far end of the valley. At best, he had an hour of daylight.

He saw his whole life a ruin from here on in. If he lived another fifty years – hardly likely – he felt he'd never get over it, abandoning the dog. He felt he was finished if he didn't find the dog. A man who would get rid of a little dog wasn't worth a damn. That kind of man would do anything, would stop at nothing.

He squirmed in the seat, kept staring into the swollen face of the sun as it moved lower into the hills. He knew the situation was all out of proportion now, but he couldn't help it. He knew he must somehow retrieve the dog, as the night before he had known he must lose it.

"I'm the one going crazy," he said and then nodded his head in agreement.

He came in the other way this time, by the field where he had let her off, alert for any sign of movement.

"Let her be there," he said.

He stopped the car and searched the field. Then he drove on, slowly. A station wagon with the motor idling was parked in the drive of the lone house, and he saw a well-dressed woman in heels come out the front door with a little girl. They stared at him as he passed. Farther on he turned left, his eyes taking in the street and the yards on each side as far down as he could see. Nothing. Two kids with bicycles a block away stood beside a parked car.

"Hi," he said to the two boys as he pulled up alongside. "You fellows see anything of a little white dog around today? A kind of white shaggy dog? I lost one."

One boy just gazed at him. The other said, "I saw a lot of little kids playing with a dog over there this afternoon. The street the other side of this one. I don't know what kind of dog it was. It was white maybe. There was a lot of kids."

"Okay, good. Thanks," Al said. "Thank you very very much," he said.

He turned right at the end of the street. He concentrated on the street ahead. The sun had gone down now. It was nearly dark. Houses pitched side by side, trees, lawns, telephone poles, parked cars, it struck him as serene, untroubled.

He could hear a man calling his children; he saw a woman in an apron step to the lighted door of her house.

"Is there still a chance for me?" Al said. He felt tears spring to his eyes. He was amazed. He couldn't help but grin at himself and shake his head as he got out his handkerchief. Then he saw a group of children coming down the street. He waved to get their attention.

"You kids see anything of a little white dog?" Al said to them.

"Oh sure," one boy said. "Is it your dog?"

Al nodded.

"We were just playing with him about a minute ago, down the street. In Terry's yard." The boy pointed. "Down the street."

"You got kids?" one of the little girls spoke up.

"I do," Al said.

"Terry said he's going to keep him. He don't have a dog," the boy said.

"I don't know," Al said. "I don't think my kids would like that. It belongs to them. It's just lost," Al said.

He drove on down the street. It was dark now, hard to see, and he began to panic again, cursing silently. He swore at what a weathervane he was, changing this way and that, one moment this, the next moment that.

He saw the dog then. He understood he had been looking at it for a time. The dog moved slowly, nosing the grass along a fence. Al got out of the car, started across the lawn, crouching forward as he walked, calling, "Suzy, Suzy, Suzy."

The dog stopped when she saw him. She raised her head. He sat down on his heels, reached out his arm, waiting. They looked at each other. She moved her tail in greeting. She lay down with her head between her front legs and regarded him. He waited. She got up. She went around the fence and out of sight.

He sat there. He thought he didn't feel so bad, all things considered. The world was full of dogs. There were dogs and there were dogs. Some dogs you just couldn't do anything with.

Collectors

I WAS OUT OF WORK. But any day I expected to hear from up north. I lay on the sofa and listened to the rain. Now and then I'd lift up and look through the curtain for the mailman.

There was no one on the street, nothing.

I hadn't been down again five minutes when I heard someone walk onto the porch, wait, and then knock. I lay still. I knew it wasn't the mailman. I knew his steps. You can't be too careful if you're out of work and you get notices in the mail or else pushed under your door. They come around wanting to talk, too, especially if you don't have a telephone.

The knock sounded again, louder, a bad sign. I eased up and tried to see onto the porch. But whoever was there was standing against the door, another bad sign. I knew the floor creaked, so there was no chance of slipping into the other room and looking out that window.

Another knock, and I said, Who's there?

This is Aubrey Bell, a man said. Are you Mr. Slater?

What is it you want? I called from the sofa.

I have something for Mrs. Slater. She's won something. Is Mrs. Slater home?

Mrs. Slater doesn't live here, I said.

Well, then, are you Mr. Slater? the man said. Mr. Slater . . . and the man sneezed.

I got off the sofa. I unlocked the door and opened it a little. He was an old guy, fat and bulky under his raincoat.

138

Water ran off the coat and dripped onto the big suitcase contraption thing he carried.

He grinned and set down the big case. He put out his hand.

Aubrey Bell, he said.

I don't know you, I said.

Mrs. Slater, he began. Mrs. Slater filled out a card. He took cards from an inside pocket and shuffled them a minute. Mrs. Slater, he read. Two-fifty-five South Sixth East? Mrs. Slater is a winner.

He took off his hat and nodded solemnly, slapped the hat against his coat as if that were it, everything had been settled, the drive finished, the railhead reached.

He waited.

Mrs. Slater doesn't live here, I said. What'd she win?

I have to show you, he said. May I come in?

I don't know. If it won't take long, I said. I'm pretty busy.

Fine, he said. I'll just slide out of this coat first. And the galoshes. Wouldn't want to track up your carpet. I see you do have a carpet, Mr. . . .

His eyes had lighted and then dimmed at the sight of the carpet. He shuddered. Then he took off his coat. He shook it out and hung it by the collar over the doorknob. That's a good place for it, he said. Damn weather, anyway. He bent over and unfastened his galoshes. He set his case inside the room. He stepped out of the galoshes and into the room in a pair of slippers.

I closed the door. He saw me staring at the slippers and said, W. H. Auden wore slippers all through China on his first visit there. Never took them off. Corns.

I shrugged. I took one more look down the street for the mailman and shut the door again.

Aubrey Bell stared at the carpet. He pulled his lips. Then he laughed. He laughed and shook his head.

What's so funny? I said.

Nothing. Lord, he said. He laughed again. I think I'm losing my mind. I think I have a fever. He reached a hand to his forehead. His hair was matted and there was a ring around his scalp where the hat had been.

Do I feel hot to you? he said. I don't know, I think I might have a fever. He was still staring at the carpet. You have any aspirin?

What's the matter with you? I said. I hope you're not getting sick on me. I got things I have to do.

He shook his head. He sat down on the sofa. He stirred at the carpet with his slippered foot.

I went to the kitchen, rinsed a cup, shook two aspirin out of a bottle.

Here, I said. Then I think you ought to leave.

Are you speaking for Mrs. Slater? he hissed. No, no, forget I said that, forget I said that. He wiped his face. He swallowed the aspirin. His eyes skipped around the bare room. Then he leaned forward with some effort and unsnapped the buckles on his case. The case flopped open, revealing compartments filled with an array of hoses, brushes, shiny pipes, and some kind of heavy-looking blue thing mounted on little wheels. He stared at these things as if surprised. Quietly, in a churchly voice, he said, Do you know what this is?

I moved closer. I'd say it was a vacuum cleaner. I'm not in the market, I said. No way am I in the market for a vacuum cleaner.

I want to show you something, he said. He took a card out of his jacket pocket. Look at this, he said. He handed me the card. Nobody said you were in the market. But look at the signature. Is that Mrs. Slater's signature or not?

I looked at the card. I held it up to the light. I turned it over, but the other side was blank. So what? I said.

Mrs. Slater's card was pulled at random out of a basket of cards. Hundreds of cards just like this little card. She has won a free vacuuming and carpet shampoo. Mrs. Slater is a winner. No strings. I am here even to do your mattress, Mr. . . . You'll be surprised to see what can collect in a mattress over the months, over the years. Every day, every night of our lives, we're leaving little bits of ourselves, flakes of this and that, behind. Where do they go, these bits and pieces of ourselves? Right through the sheets and into the mattress, *that's* where! Pillows, too. It's all the same.

He had been removing lengths of the shiny pipe and joining the parts together. Now he inserted the fitted pipes into the hose. He was on his knees, grunting. He attached some sort of scoop to the hose and lifted out the blue thing with wheels.

He let me examine the filter he intended to use.

Do you have a car? he asked.

No car, I said. I don't have a car. If I had a car I would drive you someplace.

Too bad, he said. This little vacuum comes equipped with a sixty-foot extension cord. If you had a car, you could wheel this little vacuum right up to your car door and vacuum the plush carpeting and the luxurious reclining seats as well. You would be surprised how much of us gets lost, how much of us gathers, in those fine seats over the years.

Mr. Bell, I said, I think you better pack up your things and go. I say this without any malice whatsoever.

But he was looking around the room for a plug-in. He found one at the end of the sofa. The machine rattled as if there were a marble inside, anyway something loose inside, then settled to a hum.

Rilke lived in one castle after another, all of his adult life. Benefactors, he said loudly over the hum of the vacuum. He seldom rode in motorcars; he preferred trains. Then look at

Voltaire at Cirey with Madame Châtelet. His death mask. Such serenity. He raised his right hand as if I were about to disagree. No, no, it isn't right, is it? Don't say it. But who knows? With that he turned and began to pull the vacuum into the other room.

There was a bed, a window. The covers were heaped on the floor. One pillow, one sheet over the mattress. He slipped the case from the pillow and then quickly stripped the sheet from the mattress. He stared at the mattress and gave me a look out of the corner of his eye. I went to the kitchen and got the chair. I sat down in the doorway and watched. First he tested the suction by putting the scoop against the palm of his hand. He bent and turned a dial on the vacuum. You have to turn it up full strength for a job like this one, he said. He checked the suction again, then extended the hose to the head of the bed and began to move the scoop down the mattress. The scoop tugged at the mattress. The vacuum whirred louder. He made three passes over the mattress, then switched off the machine. He pressed a lever and the lid popped open. He took out the filter. This filter is just for demonstration purposes. In normal use, all of this, this *material*, would go into your bag, here, he said. He pinched some of the dusty stuff between his fingers. There must have been a cup of it.

He had this look to his face.

It's not my mattress, I said. I leaned forward in the chair and tried to show an interest.

Now the pillow, he said. He put the used filter on the sill and looked out the window for a minute. He turned. I want you to hold onto this end of the pillow, he said.

I got up and took hold of two corners of the pillow. I felt I was holding something by the ears.

Like this? I said.

He nodded. He went into the other room and came back with another filter.

How much do those things cost? I said.

Next to nothing, he said. They're only made out of paper and a little bit of plastic. Couldn't cost much.

He kicked on the vacuum and I held tight as the scoop sank into the pillow and moved down its length – once, twice, three times. He switched off the vacuum, removed the filter, and held it up without a word. He put it on the sill beside the other filter. Then he opened the closet door. He looked inside, but there was only a box of Mouse-Be-Gone.

I heard steps on the porch, the mail slot opened and clinked shut. We looked at each other.

He pulled on the vacuum and I followed him into the other room. We looked at the letter lying face down on the carpet near the front door.

I started toward the letter, turned and said, What else? It's getting late. This carpet's not worth fooling with. It's only a twelve-by-fifteen cotton carpet with no-skid backing from Rug City. It's not worth fooling with.

Do you have a full ashtray? he said. Or a potted plant or something like that? A handful of dirt would be fine.

I found the ashtray. He took it, dumped the contents onto the carpet, ground the ashes and cigarettes under his slipper. He got down on his knees again and inserted a new filter. He took off his jacket and threw it onto the sofa. He was sweating under the arms. Fat hung over his belt. He twisted off the scoop and attached another device to the hose. He adjusted his dial. He kicked on the machine and began to move back and forth, back and forth over the worn carpet. Twice I started for the letter. But he seemed to anticipate me, cut me off, so to speak, with his hose and his pipes and his sweeping and his sweeping. . . .

★   ★   ★

143

I took the chair back to the kitchen and sat there and watched him work. After a time he shut off the machine, opened the lid, and silently brought me the filter, alive with dust, hair, small grainy things. I looked at the filter, and then I got up and put it in the garbage.

He worked steadily now. No more explanations. He came out to the kitchen with a bottle that held a few ounces of green liquid. He put the bottle under the tap and filled it.

You know I can't pay anything, I said. I couldn't pay you a dollar if my life depended on it. You're going to have to write me off as a dead loss, that's all. You're wasting your time on me, I said.

I wanted it out in the open, no misunderstanding.

He went about his business. He put another attachment on the hose, in some complicated way hooked his bottle to the new attachment. He moved slowly over the carpet, now and then releasing little streams of emerald, moving the brush back and forth over the carpet, working up patches of foam.

I had said all that was on my mind. I sat on the chair in the kitchen, relaxed now, and watched him work. Once in a while I looked out the window at the rain. It had begun to get dark. He switched off the vacuum. He was in a corner near the front door.

You want coffee? I said.

He was breathing hard. He wiped his face.

I put on water and by the time it had boiled and I'd fixed up two cups he had everything dismantled and back in the case. Then he picked up the letter. He read the name on the letter and looked closely at the return address. He folded the letter in half and put it in his hip pocket. I kept watching him. That's all I did. The coffee began to cool.

It's for a Mr. Slater, he said. I'll see to it. He said, Maybe I will skip the coffee. I better not walk across this carpet. I just shampooed it.

That's true, I said. Then I said, You're sure that's who the letter's for?

He reached to the sofa for his jacket, put it on, and opened the front door. It was still raining. He stepped into his galoshes, fastened them, and then pulled on the raincoat and looked back inside.

You want to see it? he said. You don't believe me?

It just seems strange, I said.

Well, I'd better be off, he said. But he kept standing there. You want the vacuum or not?

I looked at the big case, closed now and ready to move on.

No, I said, I guess not. I'm going to be leaving here soon. It would just be in the way.

All right, he said, and he shut the door.

Tell the Women We're Going

BILL JAMISON HAD ALWAYS been best friends with Jerry Roberts. The two grew up in the south area, near the old fairgrounds, went through grade school and junior high together, and then on to Eisenhower, where they took as many of the same teachers as they could manage, wore each other's shirts and sweaters and pegged pants, and dated and banged the same girls – whichever came up as a matter of course.

Summers they took jobs together – swamping peaches, picking cherries, stringing hops, anything they could do that paid a little and where there was no boss to get on your ass. And then they bought a car together. The summer before their senior year, they chipped in and bought a red '54 Plymouth for $325.

They shared it. It worked out fine.

But Jerry got married before the end of the first semester and dropped out of school to work steady at Robby's Mart.

As for Bill, he'd dated the girl too. Carol was her name, and she went just fine with Jerry, and Bill went over there every chance he got. It made him feel older, having married friends. He'd go over there for lunch or for supper, and they'd listen to Elvis or to Bill Haley and the Comets.

But sometimes Carol and Jerry would start making out right with Bill still there, and he'd have to get up and excuse himself and take a walk to Dezorn's Service Station to get some Coke because there was only the one bed in the apartment, a hide-away that came down in the living room. Or sometimes Jerry and Carol would head off to the bathroom, and Bill would have to move to the kitchen and pretend to be interested in the cupboards and the refrigerator and not trying to listen.

So he stopped going over so much; and then June he graduated, took a job at the Darigold plant, and joined the National Guard. In a year he had a milk route of his own and was going steady with Linda. So Bill and Linda would go over to Jerry and Carol's, drink beer, and listen to records.

Carol and Linda got along fine, and Bill was flattered when Carol said that, confidentially, Linda was "a real person."

Jerry liked Linda too. "She's great," Jerry said.

When Bill and Linda got married, Jerry was best man. The reception, of course, was at the Donnelly Hotel, Jerry and Bill cutting up together and linking arms and tossing off glasses of spiked punch. But once, in the middle of all this happiness, Bill looked at Jerry and thought how much older Jerry looked, a lot older than twenty-two. By then Jerry was the happy father of two kids and had moved up to assistant manager at Robby's, and Carol had one in the oven again.

They saw each other every Saturday and Sunday, sometimes oftener if it was a holiday. If the weather was good, they'd be over at Jerry's to barbecue hot dogs and turn the kids loose in the wading pool Jerry had got for next to nothing, like a lot of other things he got from the Mart.

Jerry had a nice house. It was up on a hill overlooking the Naches. There were other houses around, but not too close. Jerry was doing all right. When Bill and Linda and Jerry and

Carol got together, it was always at Jerry's place because Jerry had the barbecue and the records and too many kids to drag around.

It was a Sunday at Jerry's place the time it happened.

The women were in the kitchen straightening up. Jerry's girls were out in the yard throwing a plastic ball into the wading pool, yelling, and splashing after it.

Jerry and Bill were sitting in the reclining chairs on the patio, drinking beer and just relaxing.

Bill was doing most of the talking – things about people they knew, about Darigold, about the four-door Pontiac Catalina he was thinking of buying.

Jerry was staring at the clothesline, or at the '68 Chevy hardtop that stood in the garage. Bill was thinking how Jerry was getting to be deep, the way he stared all the time and hardly did any talking at all.

Bill moved in his chair and lighted a cigarette.

He said, "Anything wrong, man? I mean, you know."

Jerry finished his beer and then mashed the can. He shrugged.

"You know," he said.

Bill nodded.

Then Jerry said, "How about a little run?"

"Sounds good to me," Bill said. "I'll tell the women we're going."

They took the Naches River highway out to Gleed, Jerry driving. The day was sunny and warm, and air blew through the car.

"Where we headed?" Bill said.

"Let's shoot a few balls."

"Fine with me," Bill said. He felt a whole lot better just seeing Jerry brighten up.

"Guy's got to get out," Jerry said. He looked at Bill. "You know what I mean?"

Bill understood. He liked to get out with the guys from the plant for the Friday-night bowling league. He liked to stop off twice a week after work to have a few beers with Jack Broderick. He knew a guy's got to get out.

"Still standing," Jerry said, as they pulled up onto the gravel in front of the Rec Center.

They went inside, Bill holding the door for Jerry, Jerry punching Bill lightly in the stomach as he went on by.

"Hey there!"

It was Riley.

"Hey, how you boys keeping?"

It was Riley coming around from behind the counter, grinning. He was a heavy man. He had on a short-sleeved Hawaiian shirt that hung outside his jeans. Riley said, "So how you boys been keeping?"

"Ah, dry up and give us a couple of Olys," Jerry said, winking at Bill. "So how you been, Riley?" Jerry said.

Riley said, "So how you boys doing? Where you been keeping yourselves? You boys getting any on the side? Jerry, the last time I seen you, your old lady was six months gone."

Jerry stood a minute and blinked his eyes.

"So how about the Olys?" Bill said.

They took stools near the window. Jerry said, "What kind of place is this, Riley, that it don't have any girls on a Sunday afternoon?"

Riley laughed. He said, "I guess they're all in church praying for it."

They each had five cans of beer and took two hours to play three racks of rotation and two racks of snooker, Riley sitting on a stool and talking and watching them play, Bill always looking at his watch and then looking at Jerry.

149

Bill said, "So what do you think, Jerry? I mean, what do you think?" Bill said.

Jerry drained his can, mashed it, then stood for a time turning the can in his hand.

Back on the highway, Jerry opened it up – little jumps of eighty-five and ninety. They'd just passed an old pickup loaded with furniture when they saw the two girls.

"Look at that!" Jerry said, slowing. "I could use some of that."

Jerry drove another mile or so and then pulled off the road. "Let's go back," Jerry said. "Let's try it."

"Jesus," Bill said. "I don't know."

"I could use some," Jerry said.

Bill said, "Yeah, but I don't know."

"For Christ's sake," Jerry said.

Bill glanced at his watch and then looked all around. He said, "You do the talking. I'm rusty."

Jerry hooted as he whipped the car around.

He slowed when he came nearly even with the girls. He pulled the Chevy onto the shoulder across from them. The girls kept on going on their bicycles, but they looked at each other and laughed. The one on the inside was dark-haired, tall, and willowy. The other was light-haired and smaller. They both wore shorts and halters.

"Bitches," Jerry said. He waited for the cars to pass so he could pull a U.

"I'll take the brunette," he said. He said, "The little one's yours."

Bill moved his back against the front seat and touched the bridge of his sunglasses. "They're not going to do anything," Bill said.

"They're going to be on your side," Jerry said.

He pulled across the road and drove back. "Get ready," Jerry said.

"Hi," Bill said as the girls bicycled up. "My name's Bill," Bill said.

"That's nice," the brunette said.

"Where are you going?" Bill said.

The girls didn't answer. The little one laughed. They kept bicycling and Jerry kept driving.

"Oh, come on now. Where you going?" Bill said.

"No place," the little one said.

"Where's no place?" Bill said.

"Wouldn't you like to know," the little one said.

"I told you my name," Bill said. "What's yours? My friend's Jerry," Bill said.

The girls looked at each other and laughed.

A car came up from behind. The driver hit his horn.

"Cram it!" Jerry shouted.

He pulled off a little and let the car go around. Then he pulled back up alongside the girls.

Bill said, "We'll give you a lift. We'll take you where you want. That's a promise. You must be tired riding those bicycles. You look tired. Too much exercise isn't good for a person. Especially for girls."

The girls laughed.

"You see?" Bill said. "Now tell us your names."

"I'm Barbara, she's Sharon," the little one said.

"All right!" Jerry said. "Now find out where they're going."

"Where you girls going?" Bill said. "Barb?"

She laughed. "No place," she said. "Just down the road."

"Where down the road?"

"Do you want me to tell them?" she said to the other girl.

"I don't care," the other girl said. "It doesn't make any

difference," she said. "I'm not going to go anyplace with anybody anyway," the one named Sharon said.

"Where you going?" Bill said. "Are you going to Picture Rock?"

The girls laughed.

"That's where they're going," Jerry said.

He fed the Chevy gas and pulled up off onto the shoulder so that the girls had to come by on his side.

"Don't be that way," Jerry said. He said, "Come on." He said, "We're all introduced."

The girls just rode on by.

"I won't bite you!" Jerry shouted.

The brunette glanced back. It seemed to Jerry she was looking at him in the right kind of way. But with a girl you could never be sure.

Jerry gunned it back onto the highway, dirt and pebbles flying from under the tires.

"We'll be seeing you!" Bill called as they went speeding by.

"It's in the bag," Jerry said. "You see the look that cunt gave me?"

"I don't know," Bill said. "Maybe we should cut for home."

"We got it made!" Jerry said.

He pulled off the road under some trees. The highway forked here at Picture Rock, one road going on to Yakima, the other heading for Naches, Enumclaw, the Chinook Pass, Seattle.

A hundred yards off the road was a high, sloping, black mound of rock, part of a low range of hills, honeycombed with footpaths and small caves, Indian sign-painting here and there on the cave walls. The cliff side of the rock faced the highway and all over it were things like this: NACHES 67 —

GLEED WILDCATS – JESUS SAVES – BEAT YAKIMA –
REPENT NOW.

They sat in the car, smoking cigarettes. Mosquitoes came in
and tried to get at their hands.

"Wish we had a beer now," Jerry said. "I sure could go
for a beer," he said.

Bill said, "Me too," and looked at his watch.

When the girls came into view, Jerry and Bill got out of the
car. They leaned against the fender in front.

"Remember," Jerry said, starting away from the car, "the
dark one's mine. You got the other one."

The girls dropped their bicycles and started up one of the
paths. They disappeared around a bend and then reappeared
again, a little higher up. They were standing there and looking down.

"What're you guys following us for?" the brunette called
down.

Jerry just started up the path.

The girls turned away and went off again at a trot.

Jerry and Bill kept climbing at a walking pace. Bill was
smoking a cigarette, stopping every so often to get a good
drag. When the path turned, he looked back and caught a
glimpse of the car.

"Move it!" Jerry said.

"I'm coming," Bill said.

They kept climbing. But then Bill had to catch his breath.
He couldn't see the car now. He couldn't see the highway,
either. To his left and all the way down, he could see a strip
of the Naches like a strip of aluminum foil.

Jerry said, "You go right and I'll go straight. We'll cut the
cockteasers off."

Bill nodded. He was too winded to speak.

He went higher for a while, and then the path began to drop, turning toward the valley. He looked and saw the girls. He saw them crouched behind an outcrop. Maybe they were smiling.

Bill took out a cigarette. But he could not get it lit. Then Jerry showed up. It did not matter after that.

Bill had just wanted to fuck. Or even to see them naked. On the other hand, it was okay with him if it didn't work out.

He never knew what Jerry wanted. But it started and ended with a rock. Jerry used the same rock on both girls, first on the girl called Sharon and then on the one that was supposed to be Bill's.

Lemonade

When he came to my house months ago to measure
my walls for bookcases, Jim Sears didn't look like a man
who'd lose his only child to the high waters
of the Elwha River. He was bushy-haired, confident,
cracking his knuckles, alive with energy, as we
discussed tiers, and brackets, and this oak stain
compared to that. But it's a small town, this town,
a small world here. Six months later, after the bookcases
have been built, delivered and installed, Jim's
father, a Mr. Howard Sears, who is "covering for his son"
comes to paint our house. He tells me – when I ask, more
out of small-town courtesy than anything, "How's Jim?" –
that his son lost Jim Jr in the river last spring.
Jim blames himself. "He can't get over it,
neither," Mr. Sears adds. "Maybe he's gone on to lose
his mind a little too," he adds, pulling on the bill
of his Sherwin-Williams cap.
  Jim had to stand and watch as the helicopter
grappled with, then lifted, his son's body from the river
with tongs. "They used like a big pair of kitchen tongs
for it, if you can imagine. Attached to a cable. But God always
takes the sweetest ones, don't He?" Mr. Sears says. "He has
His own mysterious purposes." "What do *you* think about it?"
I want to know. "I don't want to think," he says. "We
can't ask or question His ways. It's not for us to know.
I just know He taken him home now, the little one."

He goes on to tell me Jim Sr.'s wife took him to thirteen foreign
countries in Europe in hopes it'd help him get over it. But
it didn't. He couldn't. "Mission unaccomplished," Howard says.
Jim's come down with Parkinson's disease. What next?
He's home from Europe now, but still blames himself
for sending Jim Jr. back to the car that morning to look for
that thermos of lemonade. They didn't need any lemonade
that day! Lord, lord, what was he thinking of, Jim Sr. has said
a hundred – no, a thousand – times now, and to anyone who will
still listen. If only he hadn't made lemonade in the first
place that morning! What could he have been thinking about?
Further, if they hadn't shopped the night before at Safeway, and
if that bin of yellowy lemons hadn't stood next to where they
kept the oranges, apples, grapefruit and bananas.
That's what Jim Sr. had really wanted to buy, some oranges
and apples, not lemons for lemonade, forget lemons, he hated
lemons – at least now he did – but Jim Jr., he liked lemonade,
always had. He wanted lemonade.

"Let's look at it this way," Jim Sr. would say, "those lemons
had to come from someplace, didn't they? The Imperial Valley,
probably, or else over near Sacramento, they raise lemons
there, right?" They had to be planted and irrigated and
watched over and then pitched into sacks by field workers and
weighed and then dumped into boxes and shipped by rail or
truck to this god-forsaken place where a man can't do anything
but lose his children! Those boxes would've been off-loaded
from the truck by boys not much older than Jim Jr. himself.
Then they had to be uncrated and poured all yellow and
lemony-smelling out of their crates by those boys, and washed
and sprayed by some kid who was still living, walking around town,
living an breathing, big as you please. Then they were carried
into the store and placed in that bin under that eye-catching sign
that said Have You Had Fresh Lemonade Lately? As Jim Sr.'s
reckoning went, it harks all the way back to first causes, back to

the first lemon cultivated on earth. If there hadn't been any lemons
on earth, and there hadn't been any Safeway store, well, Jim would
still have his son, right? And Howard Sears would still have his
grandson, sure. You see, there were a lot of people involved
in this tragedy. There were the farmers and the pickers of lemons,
the truck drivers, the big Safeway store . . . Jim Sr., too, he was
    ready
to assume his share of responsibility, of course. He was the most
guilty of all. But he was still in his nosedive, Howard Sears
told me. Still, he had to pull out of this somehow and go on.
Everybody's heart was broken, right. Even so.

Not long ago Jim Sr.'s wife got him started in a little
wood-carving class here in town. Now he's trying to whittle bears
and seals, owls, eagles, seagulls, anything, but
he can't stick to any one creature long enough to finish
the job, is Mr. Sears's assessment. The trouble is, Howard Sears
goes on, every time Jim Sr. looks up from his lathe, or his
carving knife, he sees his son breaking out of the water downriver,
and rising up – being reeled in, so to speak – beginning to turn and
turn in circles until he was up, way up above the fir trees, tongs
sticking out of his back, and then the copter turning and swinging
upriver, accompanied by the roar and whap-whap of
the chopper blades. Jim Jr. passing now over the searchers who
line the bank of the river. His arms are stretched out from his sides,
and drops of water fly out from him. He passes overhead once more,
closer now, and then returns a minute later to be deposited, ever
so gently laid down, directly at the feet of his father. A man
who, having seen everything now – his dead son rise from the river
in the grip of metal pinchers and turn and turn in circles flying
above the tree line – would like nothing more now than
to just die. But dying is for the sweetest ones. And he remembers
sweetness, when life was sweet, and sweetly
he was given that other lifetime.